He released her and stepped back, breathing harshly. 'I told you this wasn't going to happen.'

Ellie crossed her arms beneath her breasts, lifting them into mouthwatering prominence, though he was sure she didn't realize it. 'You're not the boss of me, Conor. We aren't kids. And I don't have to take orders from you. I've been running my own life just fine.'

'Quit flirting with me,' he demanded, already undressing her in his head. Two things held him back. First, the memory of her dead husband. A year and a half wasn't long enough to work through that kind of grief. And second, the memory of how a younger Ellie had judged him and found him wanting.

And still, it was damned hard to resist her.

Second Chance with the Billionaire

JANICE
MAYNARD

First published in Great Britain 2015
by Mills & Boon, an imprint of Harlequin (UK) Limited,
Large Print edition 2015
Eton House, 18-24 Paradise Road,
Richmond, Surrey, TW9 1SR

ISBN: 978-0-263-26042-7

Harlequin (UK) Limited's policy is to use papers that are natural, renewable and recyclable products and made from wood grown in sustainable forests. The logging and manufacturing processes conform to the legal environmental regulations of the country of origin.

Printed and bound in Great Britain
by CPI Antony Rowe, Chippenham, Wiltshire

JANICE MAYNARD

is a *USA TODAY* bestselling author who lives in beautiful east Tennessee with her husband. She holds a BA from Emory and Henry College and an MA from East Tennessee State University. In 2002 Janice left a fifteen-year career as an elementary school teacher to pursue writing full-time. Now her first love is creating sexy, character-driven, contemporary romance stories.

Janice loves to travel and enjoys using those experiences as settings for books. Hearing from readers is one of the best perks of the job! Visit her website, janicemaynard.com, and follow her on Facebook and Twitter.

For all of you who remember
the sweet rush of young love…
sometimes it lasts forever.

One

Conor Kavanagh had been antsy ever since he heard Ellie Porter was back in town. In spite of the many celebrities and moguls who vacationed here, Silver Glen, North Carolina, wasn't all that big a place. Chances were he'd bump into her sooner or later.

The notion gave him goose bumps. But not the good kind. Ellie Porter was part of his past. A fantasy. A regret. A deep hurt he'd buried beneath layers of indifference. He didn't need the ghost of girlfriends past to tell him he'd messed up.

Hell, he'd made more mistakes in his almost-thirty years than a lot of people made in a lifetime. But he liked to think he'd learned from them. Besides, Ellie wasn't an old girlfriend. At least not in reality. He'd kissed her once, but that was it.

In the privacy of his imagination, however, he'd done a lot more. Ellie had featured in his adolescent fantasies on a nightly basis. He'd been head over heels, hormone driven, wildly in lust with her. Everything about her reduced him to shivering need.

The smell of her hair. The dimple in her cheek when she smiled. The way her breasts filled out a sweater. Even the tiny gap between her two front teeth had charmed him. He would have given his family's entire fortune for the chance to spend one night with her. To lose himself in her soft, beautiful body and show her how much he cared.

But Ellie Porter and her twin brother, Kirby, had been his two best friends in the whole wide world. So Conor had kept his daydreams to himself, and never once had he let on to Kirby that he thought of Ellie as far more than a pal, even after he'd finally kissed his buddy's sister.

She'd been popular in high school. A long list of guys had panted after her. Probably even entertained the same fantasies that kept Conor awake and hard at night. Each time she went out with a new date, Conor suffered. He wanted to be the one to hold doors for her and put an arm around her in the movie theater and walk her home on warm, scented summer nights.

But though he and Ellie had shared an undefinable *something* that went beyond mere friendship, Ellie had disapproved of Conor's risk-taking. Her rejection of an integral part of his personality had ended anything romantic almost before it began.

He'd often wondered what might have happened if the Porters had stayed in Silver Glen. Would Conor ever have persuaded Ellie to give him another chance? It was a question with no answer. And now they had both moved on. Ellie was married. Conor was still the guy who pitted himself against danger to prove he was alive.

Loud laughter at the table behind him startled him out of his reverie. The Silver Dollar Saloon was a rowdy place on the weekends. His brother Dylan owned the upscale honky-tonk. It wasn't unusual to see the second-born Kavanagh behind the bar dispensing drinks and advice and jokes along with the pretzels and booze.

Dylan was an extrovert and a people person. He'd settled down a lot since marrying Mia and adopting little Cora. You might even call him a family man. But he still loved the Silver Dollar.

Conor couldn't blame him. It was the kind of place where everybody knew your name. Locals and tourists alike were drawn to its atmosphere of camaraderie and fun. The music was good, the service above par and the burgers legendary.

Dylan made his way down to the end of the bar and stood in front of Conor, raising an eyebrow at the half-empty bottle of beer Conor had been nursing for the better part of an hour. "I'm losing money on you," he said. "You're not eating, you're not drinking. If I didn't know better, I'd think you were in love."

Conor finished off his beer and grimaced. "God forbid. Just because you're all gaga over marital bliss doesn't mean the rest of us have to follow suit. I'm perfectly happy as a single man. I like my freedom."

"You don't know what you're missing."

Dylan's smug assurance was designed to get a rise out of Conor, but it didn't work. Because deep down, Conor knew it was the truth. He'd seen his older brothers, one by one, succumb to Cupid's mischief, and the reality of the situation was, they were all happier than Conor had ever seen them.

Liam and Zoe, Dylan and Mia, Aidan and Emma. Even Gavin, who was a hermit and a curmudgeon at times, had been tripped up by the gorgeous and bubbly Cass.

So, yeah…it was hard to overlook the self-satisfied arrogance of his siblings, who were getting laid on a nightly basis. They practically oozed testosterone and caveman triumph.

But what really got to Conor was the look in their eyes when they were with their wives. When they thought no one was watching. Those moments when the alpha males softened and Conor could see the wealth of love that bonded each man with his spouse. That kind of connection was rare and wonderful and Conor would be lying if he said he wasn't the tiniest bit envious.

It wasn't in the cards for Conor, though. The one female who had ever inspired such a depth of feeling in him had dealt him a rejection that was very personal. Ellie had disapproved of his love for courting danger. In spite of his attempt to be honest with her and to explain why skiing was so important to him, he'd lost her, anyway.

Ellie had wanted Conor to change who he was. She'd begged him to be more careful. And in the end, she had stood by his hospital bed with sorrow in her eyes and told him they didn't have a future, because he loved the rush of adrenaline more than he cared about her.

Even then he had seen the truth in her words. As a child, he'd suffered from a respiratory ailment that kept him confined indoors. Once he finally outgrew the problem, he'd been determined to prove himself. He was driven to be the fastest and best at everything he did.

That blind determination to be number one had cost him.

Life was full of regrets. He should know. A man had to move forward or be forever cemented in the past. Personally and professionally, he'd had plenty of opportunities to learn that lesson the hard way.

Dylan handed him a menu. "Buy something. Flirt with someone. You're giving the place a bad vibe."

With a reluctant grin, Conor shook his head. "God forbid that you should let your brother hang out undisturbed. Bring me a Coke and a cheeseburger, damn it."

Dylan nodded, his attention drawn to the two men arguing heatedly at table six. "That's more like it."

When Dylan strode away to break up the potentially violent situation, Conor watched the interaction with admiration. Somehow his brother managed to steer both men to the front door and outside without causing a fuss. The Silver Dollar didn't tolerate brawls.

While Conor waited for his food, he flipped through messages on his cell phone and frowned, not really seeing any of them. What would happen if he simply showed up at Ellie's front door and said hello? Would she look the same? Would he like her as much?

They hadn't seen each other in thirteen years, or was it fourteen by now? She wouldn't be sixteen anymore. So why did he still see her that way? It made no sense. All he was doing was torturing himself with one of those weird good-old-days memories that never held up under scrutiny.

Like the octogenarian who goes back to his childhood home only to find a strip mall where he used to play, Conor was keeping alive something that wasn't even real. Memories were not bad things. As long as you realized that the only truth was the moment you were living right now.

His accident years ago had cost him a skiing career. And had erased any possibility of having Ellie Porter in his life. Those two facts were irrefutable.

And what about Kirby? Conor and Kirby had been closer than brothers. They had studied together and played sports together and dreamed dreams together. Both of them had had big plans for the future. But their bond had been broken by something as mundane as Kirby's parents taking him to another hemisphere.

Could a friendship like that be resurrected? Only time would tell...but Conor hoped so.

He finished his meal and yawned despite the fact that it was not even ten o'clock yet. He'd been up at dawn. Had worked his ass off all day. He was the boss. He *owned* the Silver Mountain Ski Resort. But idle living had never suited him. Maeve Kavanagh had raised seven sons, mostly unassisted, and in spite of the Kavanagh fortune and the family's influence and reach in the town of Silver Glen, she had drilled into her boys the value of hard work.

According to Conor's mother, the size of a man's bank balance was no excuse for laziness. Her boys heeded the message. Liam ran the Silver Beeches Lodge with his mother. Dylan owned and managed the Silver Dollar Saloon. Aidan was some kind of banking genius up in New York. Gavin's baby was the Silver Eye, his cyber security operation.

On Conor's twenty-third birthday, he had officially taken over the ski resort. The move seemed obvious since he had spent a large portion of his childhood and adolescence gliding down those slopes. At one time he had dreamed of medals and podiums and national anthems being played in his honor.

But life had a way of smacking you in the face occasionally. His plans had changed.

Conor had a *good* life. And a great family. He was a lucky man.

So why did he still think about Ellie Porter?

The two blondes at table six were giving him the eye. They were both cute and looked athletic. No doubt, exactly his type. But tonight he couldn't summon up enough interest to play their game, even with a threesome in the realm of possibility. What in the hell was wrong with him?

"Conor?" He felt a hand on his shoulder.

Summoning a smile, he turned on his stool, prepared to make an excuse…to say he was leaving. But dark blue eyes stopped him in his tracks. "Ellie?"

She nodded, her expression guarded. "Yes. It's me. I need to talk to you."

Ellie found herself at a distinct disadvantage when Conor stood up. She had always been barely five foot five, and Conor Kavanagh was a long, tall drink of water, several inches over six feet. The pale gold highlights in his dark blond hair were the result of many hours spent outdoors. Women paid a lot of money to get that look in a salon.

He wore his hair shorter than he had as a kid. But it was still far too gorgeous for a guy. Not fair at all. The only thing that saved his face from being classically handsome was the silvery scar that ran up the side of his chin and along his jawline. When he was twelve, he'd fallen off the ski lift and cut his face open on a rock.

She and Kirby had been in the seat behind him and had watched in horror as the snow below turned red with Conor's blood. But Conor had jumped up and waved at them, his typical devil-may-care attitude in full view. Even now, the memory made her queasy.

Conor had definitely grown into his looks.

His rangy frame was much the same as she remembered, though with more muscles, a few more pounds and a posture that said he was at ease in his own skin. The extra weight suited him. Back in high school he'd been on the thin side.

His passion for sports, skiing in particular, and his high-speed metabolism had made it difficult for him to take in enough calories. For Ellie, who had always battled her weight, his problem was one she would have gladly handled.

He stared at her without smiling, the expression in his gray eyes inscrutable. "I heard you and Kirby were back in town."

She nodded, feeling vaguely guilty. Should she have called Conor instead of simply showing up? "Grandpa isn't doing well. Kirby and I came home to look after him until my parents retire in nine months. They've opened their last clinic in Bolivia, so once it's up and running to their satisfaction, they'll move back to Silver Glen."

"I see."

Conor's reticence bothered her. At one time, she and Kirby and Conor had been thick as thieves, their friendship unbreakable. But then her parents had done the unthinkable. They'd become medical missionaries and had moved their family to the jungles of South America to dispense health care to the people there.

"We missed you," she said quietly. Even before the move, she and Conor had parted ways.

Conor shrugged. "Yeah. But it's a hell of a long way from Silver Glen to Bolivia. It's not surprising that we lost touch."

She nodded. For several months emails had winged back and forth between Kirby and Conor. The occasional snail-mail letter. But in the end, she and Kirby had been too far removed from their old life to maintain that thread. And Ellie had been too hurt by Conor's pigheadedness to write.

"We were furious, you know," she said. "In the

beginning. We begged my parents to let us stay here with Grandpa and enjoy our senior year."

"I remember."

"But they insisted that the four of us were a family. And that we needed to stick together."

Conor shifted his weight, looking beyond her. "Let's grab a table," he said. "Have you had dinner?"

"Yes." She followed him and took the chair he held out for her.

"Then how about a piece of lemon pie? Dylan swears it's the best in the state."

"That sounds great." She rarely ate desserts, but tonight she needed something to occupy her hands and some activity to fill the awkward silences. In her head, she had imagined this meeting going far differently.

Conor's lack of enthusiasm for their reunion threw her. When they had placed their order, he leaned his chair back on two legs and eyed her unsmiling. "You've turned into a beautiful woman, Ellie. And that's saying something, because back in high school you were the prettiest thing I'd ever seen."

She gaped, totally taken off guard. Heat flooded her cheeks. "You're being kind."

"Not kind…merely truthful," he said, his expression guarded. "I was a guy, not a eunuch. Being your friend wasn't always easy."

Still that undercurrent of *something*.

"Are you angry with me?" she asked, not at all sure what was going on.

"No. Not now."

"But once upon a time?"

"Yeah. I guess I thought both you and Kirby could have argued harder to stay."

She bit her lip. "You don't know the half of it," she said softly, regret giving her an inward twinge. "We were typical sullen teenagers when we didn't get our own way. We yelled and pleaded and sulked. But Mom and Dad insisted we were a family and that we would be leaving the nest soon enough…that we needed to stick together. The thing is, they were right. Kirby and I had the most amazing experiences that year."

"What about your studies?"

"They homeschooled us. And we worked in the clinic. I wish you could have been there, Conor.

The jungle is an incredible place. Dangerous, of course, but so beautiful."

"I'm glad things worked out." When he glanced at his watch, she sensed he was impatient.

Sadness filled her chest. At one time this man had known all her secrets. Had been at her side for most of the important moments of her life.

"How about a dance?" she said impulsively. "For old times' sake."

His body language was one big negative, but he nodded. "If you want to."

The small dance floor was crowded with other couples. Conor held her close and moved them across the scarred hardwood with ease. Gone was the slightly gawky boy she had known. In his place was a powerful, confident man. Not that the young Conor had ever *lacked* confidence, but still…this Conor was different.

Her response to him took her by surprise. The sexual awareness might be a weak remnant of the past, but then again, she was a living, breathing woman, and Conor was masculinity personified. She'd come here tonight to plead her brother's case. Ending up in Conor's arms was both unsettling and frightening. She didn't have the right to revel in his embrace.

He smelled like an ad for expensive men's after-shave, but more on the faint and tantalizing end than the knock-you-down way some guys bathed in it. Conor was both achingly familiar and at the same time almost a stranger. The dichotomy was one she couldn't explain.

Her sundress left her shoulders bare. Conor had one hand at her waist and with the other, clasped her fingers in his. She wondered if he experienced the tingling that rocked her.

Over the years, she had thought of him, of course. Wondered how he was doing. But she didn't remember ever feeling this *aware* of his male appeal, even as a giddy teenage girl with a crush.

When the song ended, they returned to their table. Conor sighed. "It's great to see you, Ellie. But you said you needed to talk to me. And so far all we've done is exchange pleasantries. It's a beautiful night. Do you want to go for a drive so we can hear ourselves think?"

The noise level in the Silver Dollar had increased exponentially as the hour advanced. Conor's offer was appealing, but she didn't have the luxury of wasting time. "That sounds wonderful, but I can't be out much longer. I have a baby, Conor…a son. I put him to bed before I came, and Kirby is keeping an eye on the baby monitor, but sometimes he wakes up."

Though Conor seemed shocked by her confession, after several beats of silence, he gave her a genuine smile. "The baby or Kirby?"

"Very funny." She didn't know why she was so nervous about saying what she needed to say. Except that she still had a hard time accepting it. "I need you to spend some time with Kirby."

Her request came out sounding more like a demand, but Conor didn't flinch. "Of course," he said calmly. "It will be fun to catch up and rehash old times."

"That's not what I meant." She felt her throat tighten with emotion. Tears stung her eyes, foolish tears, because she'd had plenty of time to come to terms with what had happened. "Kirby needs you," she said. "He's had a huge blow, and I think it will help him to talk to you."

"Why me?" Conor's terse question echoed suspicion.

She couldn't blame him. He must wonder why no one else in her life had stepped forward to lend support. Conor been invited to her wedding by Kirby, but he'd sent his regrets along with an impersonal gift card. The fourteen years were an enormous void filled with only the slightest contacts from either side.

She rubbed her temples with forefingers. "You had a phenomenal future ahead of you as a competitive skier. Everyone knew it. You had made the American team as a not-quite sixteen-year-old. Everything you ever wanted was in reach."

"And then I blew out my knee." The words were flat.

"Yes. So you lost that dream and had to learn who you were without it."

"No offense, Ellie, but I'd just as soon not rehash that year."

"Sorry." She knew what it had cost him to give up his life's goal. The doctors had told him he could ski cautiously, but that if he tried to hit the slopes aggressively enough to win championships, he risked losing all mobility in his right leg. Despite the overwhelming disappointment, Conor had sucked it up and gotten on with his life.

"What's wrong with Kirby? What happened?"

She wiped the tears away, not embarrassed but feeling painfully vulnerable. "He lost a foot. Had it amputated just above the ankle."

Two

Conor's stomach clenched. "*Jesus*, Ellie." *Stunned* didn't come close to describing how he felt. The Kirby Conor had known could do anything. He'd played football, basketball and, though he wasn't a fanatic like Conor, he'd been a creditable skier. "Tell me..." He swallowed hard, not at all sure he really wanted to know.

Ellie was pale, her eyes haunted. "He finished medical school and his residency eighteen months ago. You would be so proud of him, Conor. He's brilliant. And as good a doctor as my parents are."

"That doesn't surprise me. He always ruined the curve for the rest of us."

Ellie nodded. "Exactly. I had to study, but Kirby could look at a textbook and remember almost everything he read."

"His brain isn't in question. What happened?"

"As a celebration, he wanted to climb Aconcagua. He went up with a group of other men, almost all of them experienced climbers. But they got caught in a freak storm. The ledge they were sheltering on broke and Kirby fell several hundred feet. His lower leg was caught between rocks. It took rescuers almost forty-eight hours to get to him."

Conor stared at her aghast, sick at the thought that Kirby survived two nights and days on the mountain only to lose part of a limb. "He's lucky to be alive."

Ellie nodded, tears glittering on her eyelashes. "He's had three surgeries and endless hours of therapy. He's walking on a prosthetic foot. But, Conor…"

He touched her hand on the table. "But what?"

"He thinks he can't be a good doctor anymore."

Conor saw how close she was to breaking down. Unbidden, old feelings rushed in. The need to protect Ellie, first and foremost. He'd always wanted to be her savior. Apparently, some things never changed. A crowded bar on a Friday night was not the place for this kind of conversation. "Come on," he said, pulling her to her feet. "I'll walk you to your car."

Outside, he took a deep breath. The night was humid…sticky. But he felt cold inside. Knowing what his friend had suffered made him angry and sad and guilty for all the times he'd grieved for his own lost career. His injury was nothing compared to what Kirby faced.

Ellie's profile in the illumination from the streetlight on the far side of the parking lot was achingly familiar. Golden-red hair slid across her shoulders. As a teenager he remembered that she always bemoaned her lack of curls. But the silky straight fall of pale auburn was perfect just as it was.

She was curvy, not thin. A very womanly female. He was assaulted with a barrage of emotions that didn't match up. Part of him wanted to explore the physical pull. But an even stronger part wanted to console her.

"I have to go," she whispered, the words barely audible.

"Come here, Ellie." He pulled her into his embrace and held her as she gave in to tears. The sobs were neither soft nor quiet. She cried as if her heart were breaking. And maybe it was. Twins experienced a special bond. Kirby's injury would have marked her, as well.

Conor stroked his hands down her back, petting her, murmuring words of comfort. Resting his chin on top of her head, he pondered the fact that after all this time, he still experienced something visceral and inescapable when it came to Ellie Porter. Holding her like this felt like coming home. And yet he was the one who had never left.

At last her burst of grief diminished. He released her immediately when she stepped back. Why wasn't her husband the one comforting her? Where was the guy?

"I'm sorry," she muttered. "I guess I've been holding all that inside, trying to put on a brave face for Kirby."

"Understandable."

"Thank you, Conor."

Was he a beast for noticing the soft curves of her cleavage above the bodice of her sundress? Or the way her waist nipped in, creating the perfect resting place for a man's hands?

"For what?"

"For listening."

He shook his head. "I'm glad you came to find me. And of course I'll spend time with Kirby. But I have more questions, and it's late. Why don't you bring the baby with you and come up to the ski lodge tomorrow? I'll even feed you."

"I don't want to intrude."

"All my guys have gone to Asheville for the weekend to catch an outdoor concert. You won't see anyone but me."

She nodded slowly. "I'd like that."

"Silver Glen has missed the Porters."

That coaxed a smile from her. "And Conor Kavanagh? What about him?"

He ran his hand down her arms, needing to touch her one last time. "Him, too," he said gruffly. "Him most of all."

Ellie drove the short distance home making sure all her attention was focused on the road. She was painfully glad Conor hadn't asked about Kevin. It would have been hard to talk about that on top of everything else. Her body trembled in the aftermath of strong emotions, and she felt so very tired. Emory was a good baby and slept well as a rule, but he was a handful. Between caring for him and looking after Kirby and her grandfather, she was running on empty.

Leaning on Conor, even briefly, had felt wonderful. He was the same strong, decent, teasing guy she had known so long ago, but even better. He carried himself with the masculine assurance of a grown man. He had been gentle with her, and kind. But something else had shimmered beneath the surface.

Surely she hadn't imagined the undercurrent of sexual awareness. On her part, it was entirely understandable. Conor was a gorgeous, appealing man in his prime. But maybe she had imagined the rest. She was exhausted and stretched to the limit and at least fifteen pounds overweight.

She couldn't even remember the last time she felt sexy and desirable. At least not until tonight. Something about the way Conor looked at her brought back memories of being a teenager and having a crush on her brother's best friend.

Many times she had envied the bond between

Kirby and Conor. Though she and her brother were closer than most siblings, there was no denying the fact that an adolescent boy needed someone of his own sex to hang out with. The two guys had included Ellie in most of their adventures. It wasn't their fault if she sometimes felt like a third wheel.

And of course, she had never let Kirby see how she felt about Conor. Not even when Conor nearly killed himself and Ellie stood in a hospital room, scared but determined as she gave Conor an ultimatum. It was one of the few secrets she had ever kept from her brother.

That, and her current fear that Kirby was going to give up.

As she pulled into the driveway of her grandfather's tidy 1950s bungalow, she took a deep breath. She gave herself a minute to stare up at the stars before going inside. Loneliness gripped her, tightening her throat. For better or for worse, she was the glue that held this household together at the moment. The burden lay heavy at times.

Inside, she found Kirby sitting in the dark, kicked back in the recliner, watching a cable news program. She turned on a small table lamp and sat down across from him, yawning.

"Hey, sis," he said. "Feel better?"

She'd told him she was going for a drive to clear her head.

"Yes, thanks. I appreciate your holding down the fort while I was gone."

No need to tell him where she had been. Not yet.

Kirby shrugged, his expression guarded. "Even I can do that when our two babies are sleeping."

"How was Grandpa?"

"Not too bad tonight. He spent an hour telling me stories about Grandma and then took himself off to bed."

"Good." An awkward silence fell. No matter how hard she tried to pretend things were normal, they were anything but. She glanced at the clock on the wall. "Can I get you anything before you go to bed? Warm milk? A snack?"

Kirby's chest rose and fell in a sigh. "No. I'm good."

But he wasn't. He'd suffered wretched insomnia since the accident. Chances were, he'd avoid his bedroom again tonight and doze in the recliner until morning.

Feeling helpless and frustrated, she stood and crossed the room. Pressing a kiss to the top of his head, she put a hand on his shoulder. "You'll call me if you need anything?"

He put his hand over hers. "Go to bed, Ellie. I'm fine."

After a quick shower, she climbed onto the old-fashioned feather mattress and lay beneath a cool cotton sheet, listening to the sounds of Emory breathing. The baby had been her salvation over the past terrible months. Her little boy was innocent and precious and totally dependent on her for care. She couldn't afford to have a breakdown or any other dramatic response to the soap opera that was her life.

She had shed her share of tears over Kirby but always in private. It was important to her that he not feel like an object of pity. Which meant she forced herself to walk a fine line between being helpful and smothering him.

Her own tragedy had been forced into the shadows, because caring for Kirby had taken precedence. Seeing Conor again made her dangerously vulnerable. Even though she had sought him out, she would have to be on guard when they were together. She didn't deserve his care and concern.

As drowsiness beckoned, she allowed herself to remember what it felt like to be close to Conor, first on the dance floor and later as he held her and comforted her. She shivered, though the room was warm. What would her life have been like if she and Conor had never argued so bitterly…if the Porters had never left Silver Glen?

It was a tantalizing question.

But the truth was, she now traversed a difficult road. Grief and fatigue could be dangerous. She should not mistake Conor's kindness for something more. Her life had not turned out according to plan. Even so, she would not wallow in self-pity. And she would not cling to a man to make it through this rough patch.

She was strong and resilient. She needed to keep her head up and her eyes on the future. The guilt she carried threatened to drag her under, and she would be mortified if Conor ever suspected the truth. His friendship would be a wonderful bonus, but only if the lines were clearly drawn. Perhaps, if he managed to coax Kirby out of the doldrums, the three of them could be the trio of friends they once were.

* * *

The following morning she fixed breakfast for the men in her life and then made sandwiches for lunch and put them in the fridge. She didn't like lying to her brother, so she had scheduled a well-baby checkup for Emory and said that she was going shopping afterward.

The doctor visit was real. Kirby wouldn't expect her back at any specific time. Fortunately, the pediatrician was on time, and the appointment went off without a hitch.

Emory was in a sunny mood. She wanted him to make a good impression on Conor, which was kind of silly, but as a relatively new mom, she was still so proud of her baby and wanted the whole world to see how special he was.

The trip to the ski resort didn't take long at all. When she pulled up in front of the large Alpine-style chalet that was command central for the winter ski crowd, Ellie was impressed. She'd spent a lot of time here in her youth, but clearly, major updates had been done over the years. The grounds and exterior were immaculate.

Conor waved her over to the door. Ellie slung a diaper bag and her purse over her shoulder and scooped up the baby. As they stepped through the double oak doors carved with fir trees and mountains, she paused to take in the lobby. Although large in scale, it had a cozy feel because of the quilted wall hangings, thick area rugs and half-a-dozen fireplaces scattered around the perimeter.

Enormous plate-glass windows afforded a view of the ski slopes below. In December it would be breathtaking. Even now, at the height of summer, it was impressive.

Conor urged her toward a mission-style sofa upholstered in crimson and navy stripes. "Have a seat. I'll round up some drinks and a snack." He paused to stare at Emory. "He's a cute kid."

"His name is Emory."

"Does he take after his dad?"

Her heart clenched. Was Conor deliberately fishing for information? If so, she wasn't ready to talk about that subject. Not yet. Maybe not ever. "I think he's beginning to look like me," she said lightly, nuzzling her nose in the baby's strawberry blond curls.

Conor stared at her and then looked back at Emory. "I suppose so."

Without knowing it, she had been holding her

breath, because when Conor walked out of the room, she exhaled, all the oxygen in her lungs escaping in one *whoosh*.

Emory was unconcerned. He squirmed in her arms, wanting to get down. He was already close to walking and proved it yet again by cruising around the edges of the coffee table with confidence. When Conor returned, Emory gave him a big, slobbery grin.

As Conor set down a tray with lemonade and shortbread, Ellie lifted an eyebrow. "Somebody's domesticated," she said teasingly.

Conor shuddered theatrically. "Not me. I have a housekeeper who looks after my place and the chalet. She apparently thinks I'm in danger of starving to death, because every time she comes to clean, I find baked goods on the kitchen counter."

"She must like you very much."

Conor shook his head ruefully. "It's not like that. She's seventy-two years old. She likes the fat paycheck I give her because it supplements her income."

"If you say so." She had a hunch that the unnamed housekeeper had a soft spot for her generous boss.

Conor sat down beside Ellie on the sofa and chuckled when Emory let go of the edge of the coffee table and sat down hard on his bottom. The baby's look of indignation was comical. "He's going to lead you a merry chase as soon as he realizes he can go anywhere and everywhere."

"Don't I know it. I've already been baby proofing my grandfather's house."

"How is Mr. Porter doing?"

"He has his good days and bad. Sometimes he puts his reading glasses in the freezer and forgets to wear pants, but with Kirby and I around, he seems happy. I think he was afraid he would have to go into a rest home, so he's being extra sweet and cooperative."

"He's lucky to have you."

"That goes both ways."

Conor leaned forward, scooping up Emory and putting him back on his feet. "There you go, little man. The world is yours."

"Or at least this table." Ellie chuckled. She was torn between being excited about her son's prowess and worried that he would hurt himself. "He has no fear. Which scares me to death."

Conor nodded, his eyes on Emory's progress. "I don't know how my mom did it. Seven boys."

"That should qualify her for sainthood."

They both laughed and, for a moment, their eyes met. Ellie looked away first, her cheeks heating.

Conor leaned forward, his elbows on his knees, his gaze trained on the floor. "Are you going to tell me about Emory's dad?"

Ellie inhaled sharply, stunned that he would ask so bluntly. But then again, Conor had never shied away from difficult conversations. "No," she said. "I don't believe I am. I came here to talk about Kirby."

She saw Conor flinch. "You've developed a hard edge, Ellie."

"I'm not a child anymore, if that's what you mean."

He shot her a look over his shoulder, his warm, masculine gaze taking in her navy tank top and khaki skirt. "I'm well aware of that, believe me." Conor must have noticed that she didn't wear a wedding ring. Was that why he felt the freedom to say such things to her?

"I believe you offered me a snack," she said calmly, though her heart was beating overtime.

Conor sat back, his wry smile rueful. "I suppose that means I'm pouring."

She corralled Emory when he seemed ready to try his luck climbing onto the sofa. "No, sweetheart. No lemonade for you. I have your sippy cup of milk right here."

Conor shook his head. "Poor kid. I'll bet you won't let him have a cookie, either."

"Of course not."

Conor laughed as he handed her a glass. "I was only kidding. Even I know a little kid isn't supposed to have sugar. How old is he? I'm guessing his first birthday is not far off."

"Ten months. He's big for his age."

"I'll bet Uncle Kirby loves him."

"He does. The two of them are sweet together."

"So tell me about Kirby. Why do you think he needs to talk to me?"

Ellie took a long drink and set down her glass, still half-full. "The last year and a half has been really hard for him. Not only losing the foot, but being a patient instead of a physician. He's used to being the one in charge, the one caring for other people. So not only has he been dealing with the changes in his physical capabilities, he's gotten it in his head that he won't be a good doctor now. He has offers waiting from at least four prestigious medical centers across the country, but he refuses to deal with them."

"I'm not a counselor, Ellie."

"I know that," she said. "But you have some inkling of what it's like to have your whole life turned upside down. You've moved on. You've made new goals. You've accepted your limitations."

Three

But had he? Had he really? Conor didn't want to admit, even to himself, that he still grieved the loss of his adolescent dreams. He'd put on a brave face for his family…pretended that he was okay with no longer competing. But deep down, a tiny kernel of futile anger remained that he'd been robbed of doing the one thing that gave him such an incredible rush of exhilaration.

"I didn't get there overnight, Ellie. Acceptance takes time. And Kirby has lost far more than I ever did."

"That's not really true, if you think about it. You had to give up competing completely. But Kirby can still be a doctor."

Her words sent shock reverberating through Conor's gut. Had all his pretending been wrong? Would it have made life easier if he'd been up-front about his grief?

He cleared his throat, stunned that a woman he hadn't seen in a decade and a half could analyze the situation so succinctly. "I'll talk to him. If you think he wants to see me. But I can't promise miracles."

"I appreciate it, Conor."

Ellie's grateful smile made him uncomfortable. She glowed this morning, no other word for it. Motherhood suited her. If Conor started hanging out at the Porter household, he would see her regularly. That was probably not a good idea given his fascination with her.

Because there was still the mystery of Emory's father.

Even so, he was drawn to her warmth and caring. Or maybe it was simply the fact that he was sexually attracted to her. She had a body that was lush and ripe. He ached to touch her, much as he had as a teenager. Only now, he knew the kind of pleasure a man and a woman could share.

Imagining Ellie in his bed was definitely not

smart. Tormenting himself was pointless. Conor hadn't changed. He still courted danger. He still relished the exhilaration of pitting himself against the elements. Which meant that Ellie would be as disapproving as ever when she found out the truth about him.

He picked up Emory and blew raspberries on his tummy, anything to distract himself from the image of Ellie's naked body. "When do you want me to see Kirby?" he asked, wincing as Emory grabbed handfuls of his hair.

"Whenever it's convenient for you. I know you have a business to run."

"In case you haven't noticed, it's the off-season. I'm not exactly tied to a desk. What if I order lunch from the deli and we pick it up on the way to your grandfather's house?"

"That would be perfect. I'd already made some sandwiches for Kirby and Grandpa and left them in the fridge, but they'll keep until tomorrow."

"You want to ride with me?"

"I can't. The car seat, you know."

"Ah. Yes. Does your grandfather still live in the same house?"

"Yes." She scooped up Emory.

"Well, in that case, I'll see you over there in half an hour."

He helped Ellie load up the car and watched as she drove away. Already he felt a connection that was stronger than it should have been given their long separation.

It occurred to him suddenly that he had asked questions about Kirby, but he still had no idea what Ellie did for a living. Though she downplayed her intelligence in comparison to her twin, he knew she had done well in school, also. The teachers had loved her.

Conor had *wanted* her. But her refusal to accept him as he was had kept his adolescent urges in check. Nothing had changed. He'd be smart to ignore this inconvenient attraction. Ellie wasn't the woman for him.

The deli was accustomed to him placing to-go orders, but they were surprised by the size of this one. The cute teenager behind the counter smiled teasingly. "Having a party, Mr. Kavanagh?" she asked.

Mr. Kavanagh? Hell, did he seem that old to this kid? "Lunch with some friends."

"We have fresh strawberry cake in the back. One that's not even sliced yet. You want a few pieces?"

"I'll buy the whole thing." Conor would take any help he could get in the way of a welcome offering. He wasn't at all sure his invitation from Ellie was going to get Kirby's stamp of approval. Men liked to hide out and lick their wounds. Kirby might not appreciate having Conor show up out of the blue.

At Mr. Porter's place, Conor parked on the street and unloaded the bags from the deli. With the cake box balanced in one arm, he made his way up the walk. The property was not in great shape. Not too surprising for an older person who didn't have the strength to handle fix-it jobs.

The paint on the house was peeling in places. He saw a section of rotting wood on a soffit. Several dead plants needed to be replaced. Even the driveway needed to be resurfaced.

Ellie and Kirby no doubt had plenty of financial resources to take care of things, but maybe Conor could offer to do a few odd jobs. It would give him an excuse to hang around, and maybe he could coax Kirby into holding the ladder or drinking a beer while he kept Conor company.

Ellie waited at the door, the baby on her hip. She looked anxious but incredibly beautiful. "I told him you're coming," she said. Her eyes were darker than usual. In their depths he saw worry.

"Point me toward the kitchen," he said. "And I'll dump all this stuff. What did he say when you told him?"

"Not much."

"Great," Conor muttered. "Does the term *busybody* mean anything to you?" He put the cold items away and leaned back against the counter. The kitchen was small and dated, but cozy and welcoming in a retro way. He and Kirby and Ellie had visited here on occasion as kids.

"That's not fair," she said, her gaze mulish as Emory yanked on a strand of her hair. "Kirby *needs* company. Even if he doesn't realize it."

"So I'm your token guinea pig?"

She shrugged. "I've done all I can do. If there's going to be a change in the status quo, I'm betting on you."

"No pressure." He was stalling, honestly scared that his longtime friend was going to kick him out after an obligatory five-minute visit. “Let’s get this over with. But if he doesn’t want me here, I’m leaving.”

“We may have to ease him into it, but I know this will be a good thing.”

“I wish I had your confidence.” What did Conor possibly have to say to a man who had lost part of a limb? Yet even amid his doubts, Conor knew he would do anything to put a smile on Ellie’s face.

Mr. Porter was napping, so Kirby was the only one in the living room when Ellie and Conor walked in. In a flash, Conor saw that Kirby had changed. More than Conor could have imagined. The teenage boy Conor remembered was a man with lines at the corners of his eyes and a tight jaw that spoke of pain suffered and battles fought.

Conor crossed the room, holding out his hand. “Hey, Kirby. It’s great to have you back in town. Don’t get up, man.”

But Kirby had already risen awkwardly to his feet, his arms outstretched. “What took you so long?”

Conor hugged him hard, feeling a reciprocal level of emotion in his friend’s embrace. “I had to pick up the food.”

After a moment, they separated. Kirby settled back in his recliner. Conor took a seat close by. Kirby shook his head. "I've missed you, buddy. More than you know." The tone in his voice said a whole lot more than his prosaic words.

Conor had only a split second to ponder his next move. He tapped Kirby's knee. "So let me see this fake foot."

"Conor!" Ellie's shocked exclamation fell into a pit of silence.

Kirby blinked in shock. His jaw worked. And then he burst out laughing. A gut-deep, hearty, belly laugh that went on and on until Conor and Ellie joined in.

Kirby wiped his eyes, his grin a shadow of his former self but a grin, nevertheless. "God, it's good to see you." He lifted his pants and extended his leg. "Carbon. Latest issue. The best money can buy."

"Comfortable?"

"Hurts like hell most of the time, but I'm getting there."

Conor stood and gave Ellie his most reassuring look. "Why don't you give us some guy time? I'll keep little Emory if you don't mind. We have to train him up right."

"God forbid," Ellie said. But she handed over her son without protest. "I'll have lunch ready in half an hour."

Kirby nodded. "Thanks, sis."

When Ellie left the room, Conor juggled the baby. He'd assumed, and rightly so, that Emory's presence would fill any awkward silences. "So how are you *really* doing?"

Kirby grimaced. "Honest to God, I don't know, Conor. Most mornings when I wake up, it still seems like a dream, until I try to stand up and forget I don't have the damned prosthesis on. I can't tell you how many times I've nearly fallen on my face."

"Ellie worries about you."

"I know. She and my parents have been great through all of this. But sometimes I feel a little bit..."

"Smothered?"

Kirby glanced at the doorway and lowered his voice. "Yes. But she's been so good to me, Conor. I don't think I would have made it without her. So how can I tell her I need some space?"

"Maybe you won't have to. You and I have years to catch up on. If we're hanging out doing stuff, Ellie will be delighted, and it will give you a chance to venture out of the nest."

"So now I'm a baby bird?"

Kirby's disgruntled expression made Conor chuckle. "Bad analogy. But seriously…what do you think of the idea?"

"I'm on board. These walls have been closing in on me."

"Good." Conor paused, feeling vaguely guilty for what he was about to do. "Ellie told me a lot about you and her parents, but she's been reticent about herself. What does she do for a living? I assume she's on maternity leave?"

"Not exactly. She has degrees in political science and international affairs. Speaks several languages. A number of years ago she began working as a cultural attaché at one of the embassies in Buenos Aires. She's brilliant, Conor. But when I had my accident, she resigned to take care of me. And then, of course, the baby came along…"

"I see." Conor did see. Ellie was devoted to her twin. Generous and compassionate. But one more question loomed. He lowered his voice, not wanting Ellie to know he was snooping. "What about her husband? Are they divorced?"

"No."

The negative sent Conor's stomach into a free fall. "Oh." Disappointment knotted his chest.

Kirby shook his head, his gaze troubled. "She didn't tell you?"

Conor frowned. "Tell me what?"

"Ellie's husband Kevin was climbing with me when I had my accident. He fell also. Died of a broken neck. Didn't even know he was going to be a father."

Ellie set the large kitchen table for four and pulled the high chair to one end. She unwrapped all the food with a raised eyebrow. Conor had spared no expense. But the Kavanaghs were extremely wealthy, so it was no surprise. Their ancestors had discovered silver in these mountains several generations ago and thus solidified the family fortunes.

The town of Silver Glen was a popular destination for celebrities and public figures who wanted to get away from it all. The charming shops and wonderful restaurants, combined with year-round recreational opportunities, appealed to a well-heeled crowd.

The advisory council had taken careful measures to limit overbuilding and to keep the Alpine flavor of the community intact. Their care paid off. The Silver Beeches Lodge and the multitude of bed-and-breakfasts in town rarely had openings unless a patron booked months in advance.

Ellie checked her watch. She had given Kirby and Conor plenty of time. Taking a moment to summon her grandfather, she then returned to the living room. "Lunch is ready," she said, glancing from her brother to his best friend. The two men appeared to be enjoying themselves. Emory was curled against Conor's chest playing with a teething ring.

The meal turned out to be an awkward affair. Ellie's grandfather floated in and out, one minute coherent, the next saying bizarre things that made Ellie sad and discouraged. It was hard to see a loved one deteriorate.

At one point, Grandpa Porter sat straight up in his ladder-back chair and pointed an accusing finger at Conor. "I remember you," he said. "You used to have a soft spot for my little granddaughter, Ellie."

Though Ellie flushed with mortification, Conor took it all in stride. "Yes sir, I did. But that was a long time ago."

Kirby intervened. "Do you want some cake, Grandpa? It's homemade."

The ruse distracted the old man, fortunately. Ellie couldn't decide what was going on with Conor. He and Kirby laughed and joked together as if they had never been apart, but Conor scarcely looked at Ellie. Fortunately, Emory demanded much of her attention.

When everyone had finished eating, Conor stood. "If you all will excuse me, I have to get back to the ski lodge. This was great. Kirby, I'll call you tomorrow and we'll make a plan."

Again, Conor avoided eye contact with Ellie. "I'll walk you out to the car," she said, miffed that he was being standoffish.

"It's not necessary."

Was it only her, or did his smile seem forced? "I know that," she said. "But I want to."

Conor didn't even pause on the front porch. He strode down the path as if he had a plane to catch and not much time to make his connection. "Bye, Ellie." He tossed the words over his shoulder, barely slowing down.

"Wait," she said, grabbing his shirtsleeve. "Tell me how Kirby sounded to you. Do you think he's okay? This was the first time I've heard him laugh like that since the accident."

Conor pulled away but came to a halt, turning to face her. "He's going to be fine, Ellie. Losing the foot has knocked the wind out of him, but he hasn't given up, if that's what you're worried about."

"I *was* worried. Thank you for coming today," she said. "And thank you for the lunch."

Conor seemed uncomfortable with her gratitude. "No problem."

Well, shoot. "Did I do something to offend you?" she asked bluntly. "You're acting weird all of a sudden."

The tiny flicker of a muscle in his cheek told her that he understood what she was saying. He stood there staring at her, his expression impassive. But his hands clenched in fists at his sides.

The sky was cloudless, the sun beaming down unforgivingly. A trickle of sweat rolled down her back. Conor's posture was like stone. He was a completely different man from the one she'd spoken with at the saloon…or even at the ski lodge.

She saw his throat work.

"I owe you an apology," he said. The words seemed ripped from his chest.

"I don't understand."

"Kirby told me about your husband. About Kevin. I'm so damned sorry, Ellie."

His sympathy caught her completely off guard, though she should have guessed at some level that Kirby would spill the beans. "Thank you." What else was there to say? She couldn't tell him how she was feeling…how she had suffered. How she *still* suffered.

"To have dealt with that and also caring for Kirby…you're a strong woman." She could swear he was anguished on her behalf. But instead of feeling warmed by his empathy, it made her want to run.

She shrugged. "I don't feel strong. Most days I feel like a juggler with too many oranges and too few hands. But I don't see why this requires an apology."

"I flirted with you. I saw you weren't wearing a wedding ring and I assumed—"

"That I was divorced," she said quickly.

He nodded, his eyes bleak. "Lord, Ellie, I never even considered the fact that you were a widow."

"Does it matter?" She was shriveling inside, actively pained at the thought of discussing Kevin with Conor Kavanagh. Her guilt consumed her. What would Conor think if he ever found out the truth…the truth that not even Kirby knew?

"Yeah," he said, the word harsh. "I'm not usually such an idiot. I hope you'll accept my apology."

"You didn't do anything wrong. I *am* single, Conor, whether I want to be or not."

He ignored her words as if she had never spoken. "I'll do what I can for Kirby. And if I can help you in any way, all you need to do is ask. You're a mother and a daughter and a sister and a granddaughter. That's a lot for anyone to handle. I'd like to make things easier for you."

"Kirby needs your help, not me." She didn't want to be Conor Kavanagh's charity case. She was lonely and afraid and confused. The thought of resurrecting her friendship with Conor had kept her going lately. Now, even that was in jeopardy.

Conor stared at her, his gaze shuttered. "I'll be in touch with Kirby. Goodbye, Ellie."

Four

Conor spent a sleepless night, largely due to his dreams. Even knowing that Ellie was a grieving widow didn't keep his subconscious from going after what it wanted in erotic, carnal vignettes. The little devil on his shoulder pointed out the opportunity to take advantage of a vulnerable woman.

He wouldn't do that. Probably. Definitely.

When he heard Ellie had come home to Silver Glen, he had visions of reconnecting with the laughing, happy sixteen-year-old girl he had known. At some level, he resented the fact that she had an entire life he knew nothing about. He wanted her to be the girl in his fantasies. The childhood friend. The innocent first love.

Even to himself he had to admit the problem with that rationale. Though he had never married, he'd had two pretty serious relationships. Both of them had ended for different reasons, but he'd been emotionally invested each time. In between, he'd sown his share of wild oats.

He liked women. The way they smelled. The way they moved. The interesting ways their minds worked.

What he didn't like was the idea of competing with a dead man.

Did that make him petty? Or simply pragmatic?

Beyond that conundrum was the knowledge that he and Ellie were not suited for each other. He was still the kind of man she had once rejected. He hadn't changed. Not really. It would be better for both of them if he kept his distance.

He called Kirby early and made arrangements to pick him up at ten. "I'll wait in the car," he said. "And keep the A/C going. It's hot as hell today."

The stalled-out weather front was unrelenting. Humidity and a scorching summer sun alternately baked and broiled the town. But the real reasons he decided not to go into the house were twofold. He didn't want to see Ellie, and he *did* want to watch Kirby walk to the car.

He sent a text when he pulled up in front of the house. Moments later, as if he had been waiting by the door, Kirby appeared on the porch. As Conor watched, the other man made his way down the walk.

To a casual observer, Kirby's legs and gait would appear normal. But Conor looked beneath the surface. He saw the effort Kirby was making to walk naturally. Instead of looking toward the car, Kirby's eyes were trained on the ground as if something might jump up at any moment to trip him and send him flying.

Conor's heart contracted in sympathy, but he knew that kind of response would be the last thing Kirby wanted. Kirby didn't need Conor's platitudes. What he needed was to feel normal.

Leaning across the passenger seat, Conor unlocked the door and shoved it open. "Climb in, my friend. We've got a full day planned."

Kirby eased his big body into the car and shut the door. His forehead was beaded with sweat and his lips pressed together in a white-rimmed line. "I'm looking forward to it," he said.

Conor drummed his hands on the steering wheel. Then he sighed. "Do you have a cane, Kirby? Do you need it?"

Kirby stared straight ahead, his tumultuous emotions etched in his body language. "Did I look that bad tottering out here?" he asked, the question clipped with frustration.

"You looked fine. Honestly. But I know you, man. You once played an entire quarter of football with a busted wrist. Today, though, we're not out to prove anything. So, tell me the truth."

"Yes and yes." Kirby's breathing was shallow, his skin clammy and pale. He dropped his head against the back of the seat and muttered an expletive under his breath.

"Do you have any objections if I go get the damned thing?"

Kirby shrugged, his eyes closed. "Knock yourself out."

Conor shouldn't have been surprised to find Ellie hovering just inside the door. She was wearing old faded jeans and a white tank top that showed off her honey-colored tan and more-than-a-C-cup breasts. "I'm here for his cane," he said. "Superman out there is trying to prove something, but I want to get him home in one piece."

Ellie nodded, relief on her face. "He's stubborn."

"I'd be the same way. In fact, I *was*," he said, thinking back to the long months after his skiing accident. "I was determined to show everybody that I was okay. That things were back to normal."

"And were they?"

Though he saw nothing but simple curiosity on her face, the question stung. "No," he said bluntly. "They weren't." He wanted to drag her into his arms and kiss her. But he couldn't. He shouldn't. Even though she smelled like vanilla and temptation.

He took the carved walnut cane and left without saying goodbye. He could barely look at Ellie now. All he could see was an image of her in another man's arms, another man's bed.

When he got back in the car and tossed the cane in the backseat, Kirby had recovered enough to give him a wry smile. "They tell me not to push it…that time is what I need. But I'm damned tired of feeling like a cripple."

"Is that how you would refer to one of your patients?" Conor started the engine.

Kirby's head shot around so fast it was amazing he didn't get whiplash. "Of course not."

"Then quit whining. Life sucks. Sometimes more than others. You've made it through the worst part. You might as well concentrate on having fun once in a while."

Kirby fell silent for the remainder of the trip to the ski resort. Had Conor offended him?

Once they arrived at the lodge, Conor was stymied at first. In ordinary circumstances, he would have asked Kirby to hike the perimeter of the property with him. As high school kids, fitness had been everything to them. That was a long time ago, though, and Kirby faced a new reality.

Kirby was a doctor, a pediatric specialist according to Ellie. All Conor had to do was persuade him that losing a foot didn't negate his training and his future.

Easier said than done. But Conor was determined to ease the grief in Ellie's eyes. She had come to Conor for help, and he would give it, even if it meant keeping his physical needs in check. He was no longer an adolescent boy with a crush on a girl. Still, his need to make Ellie happy had apparently survived the years of separation.

After a quick tour of the lodge, Conor made a snap decision. If they couldn't hike the property, they could at least see it from the air. "How about riding the chairlift with me?" he said. "We run it at least once a week to see if any problems crop up."

Kirby nodded, his mood hard to read. "Sure."

At the top of the lift, Conor elbowed his friend. "If that foot falls off, I'm not crawling all over this mountain to find it."

Apparently he hit just the right note, because Kirby chuckled. "Is nothing sacred to you?"

"If you were expecting me to baby you like Ellie does, you're in for a disappointment. You lost a foot. But you're still Kirby Porter. So get over yourself."

Truth be told, Conor was a bit anxious about how Kirby would hop up on the lift. But the other man managed the quick maneuver without incident. Once they were airborne, Conor relaxed.

Except for college, Conor had spent his entire life in Silver Glen. He loved the town, the valley and especially this mountain. He'd skied his first bunny slope the winter he was three years old. After that nothing had stopped him. Until the accident over a decade later.

When the doctors told him he could no longer compete, Conor had been wrapped in a black cloud of despair. He liked nothing better than pitting himself against an unforgiving mountain. Better yet, alongside other guys just like himself who had something to prove. Skiing was the way he released the fount of energy that kept him restless and active.

Ellie had visited him in the hospital and given him a choice. Either give up skiing, or give up her. They'd been on the verge of making their mutual attraction an official *dating* relationship.

In the end, though, Conor had lost almost everything. He'd had no choice but to adapt. No more black diamond descents. No more breakneck speeds. He'd had to find another outlet for his competitive nature.

Conor didn't think he was the only one who relaxed as they rode. But it was all the way down and back up and down again before Kirby spoke.

"Thank you, Conor," he said.

"For letting you ride the lift without a ticket?"

Kirby grinned, his face in profile. “For reminding me not to be a jackass.”

“I don’t mean to minimize what you’ve been through. I know it’s been hell.”

Kirby sobered. “I thought I understood the will to live. My parents are doctors. *I’m* a doctor. But it wasn’t until I spent two entire days thinking I was going to die that I truly grasped what it means to fight for life.” He paused. “I still have nightmares. It scares Ellie.”

Conor inhaled sharply, imagining softhearted Ellie bearing witness to her twin’s demons. “She’s a strong woman.”

“You have no idea. In those early days she never left my bedside. Sometimes she would throw up in a trash can because the morning sickness was so bad.”

“And the funeral? Her husband?”

“His parents planned the whole thing. Ellie left the hospital…attended the service…and immediately came back to my room. It worries me that she hasn’t had a chance to grieve. I’m afraid that one day she’ll wake up and everything will come crashing down on her. Postpartum depression alone is dangerous. Ellie lost her husband on top of that."

"Does she talk about him?"

"Never. At first I thought she was angry because I invited Kevin to go on the climb with me. In fact, I even asked her if that was true."

"And what did she say?"

"She never answered me. It's like she's shoved his memory into a box she won't open."

"So she can concentrate on you."

"Exactly. We're close, Ellie and I, but you know that already. I've always been able to understand what she's thinking. Until now. Suddenly it's as if she's determined to forget the accident completely."

"Maybe that's the only way she can cope. Maybe it's too painful."

"I suppose so. But it's not good for her. She's given up her career. She's lost her marriage. And Lord knows, babies require the ultimate self-sacrifice. I've tried to get her to take some time for herself. To go away for a few days or get a massage. Anything. But she won't listen."

"Maybe I can think of something." Conor

winced in astonishment as the impetuous words left his lips.

Kirby turned his head. “Like what?”

“Well…” His brain scrambled for answers. “In two weeks Mom and Liam are hosting a Christmas in August ball at the Silver Beeches Lodge. It’s a fun thing they started doing three years ago. Brings in tons of extra visitors, plus, the townspeople are invited. Everyone dresses up. They’ll have a 1940s band that plays Christmas songs. It’s actually pretty fun. You could both come with me.”

Kirby shook his head. “I want to do this for her—I’ll stay at the house and look after Emory and Grandpa. That way Ellie will be more inclined to have a good time.”

“Okay.” Damn. Conor didn’t want this to look like a date. Several times in his life he’d jockeyed with another guy to win a girl’s affections. Sometimes he won, sometimes he lost.

But he was smart enough to know that going head-to-head with a ghost would be hell on a man’s ego. He’d never met Kevin. And now he never would.

Kirby mentioned the guy as if he’d been a good

husband. Conor was good at skiing. That was about it. Well, he was good in bed, too. But that wasn't likely to come into play.

He would take the grieving widow to a party and show her a fun time. That was where it ended.

Still, there was one more thing he had promised Ellie. And having her brother as a captive audience at the moment meant he could fulfill that pledge. "Ellie tells me you have some good job offers."

Kirby scowled. "All of which came in *before* I took a header off that mountainside."

"Is that a problem? You didn't get a concussion…right? You still remember all that stuff they taught you in med school, don't you?"

"There's more to being a doctor than what you read in books."

"Sure there is. Compassion. Empathy. You've lived through a traumatic experience. I'd say both of those qualities make you a better medical professional."

"It's not as simple as that, Conor."

The curt note in Kirby's voice told Conor he had pushed enough for the moment. The chairlift approached the lodge for the third time. "You ready for some lunch?" Conor asked, preparing to lend a hand if Kirby stumbled while getting off.

But his friend managed unassisted. "I could eat," Kirby said.

"I think I can scare up some leftovers and a couple of beers."

Over a meal consumed standing up in the kitchen, Conor was relieved to find out that he hadn't alienated his buddy. In fact, Kirby used the opportunity to turn the tables.

The other man crumpled an empty potato chip bag and tossed it in the garbage. "So tell me, Conor. Now that you can't go hell-for-leather down a mountainside anymore, how do you get your kicks?"

"You really want to know?"

"I asked, didn't I?"

Conor hesitated. Was his answer going to send his friend into an emotional tailspin? Conor was no shrink. But even he could see the irony. "I've taken up mountain climbing," he said.

Kirby's gaze sharpened. "Are you serious?"

Conor nodded. "Yeah…"

"Which ones?"

"I started with Whitney. Did Kilimanjaro two years ago and Everest last year."

"Damn. I wish I had known. We could have done some peaks together." He stopped suddenly, and Conor saw the exact moment his friend acknowledged that there would be no more hazardous mountains in his future.

It was a damned shame.

"I'm sorry, Kirby."

Kirby shrugged. "Adrenaline junkies have short life spans."

"Is that what you think we are?"

"It's who we used to be. I doubt either one of us has changed all that much." He paused. "So what's next?"

Conor leaned a hip against the industrial stainless steel counter. "I have plans to do Aconcagua this winter."

Kirby stared at him, jaw dropped. "Well, hell."

"Exactly."

"For God's sake, don't tell Ellie."

"I won't. But is this where you try to talk me out of going?"

Conor had been half expecting this moment ever since he heard Kirby's accident had happened on the very mountain in Argentina that Conor was slated to climb next.

Kirby shook his head slowly. "I wouldn't do that. Aconcagua is a phenomenal experience. I'm happy for you."

Conor felt a slither of unease. "You'd still call it phenomenal? After everything that happened?" In Kirby's position, how would Conor feel? The mountain had nearly killed Ellie's beloved twin. And it *had* killed his brother-in-law.

"It was a great trip," Kirby said, his jaw outthrust stubbornly.

"Right up until the part where Aconcagua kicked your ass."

"A freak accident. Could have happened to anyone."

"Mountain climbing is a dangerous venture. You knew the risks."

"And I did it, anyway."

"I get the feeling you're conflicted about that choice."

Kirby flexed his foot, the prosthetic one, his face grim and drawn. "I chose to go. It was my decision."

"And now you're paying. Is that it? You have

to give up your career because you did this to yourself?"

"Damn it, Conor…"

Conor sighed, shaking his head. "You're wearing a hair shirt, Kirby. For no reason at all. The only thing that's changed is the way your shoe fits. Nothing's gonna hold you back but you."

After a taut, lengthy silence, Kirby sighed, shaking his head. "I can't decide if you're my therapist or my cheerleader, but it's creeping me out. Can we call a moratorium on talking about my situation?"

"Only if you promise to quit acting like a pathetic loser."

Kirby grinned, ending the verbal standoff. "Did I mention that I'm glad to see you again?"

Conor cuffed him on the shoulder, careful not to make him stumble. "Don't get all mushy on me."

"Moron."

"Half-wit."

"I can do this all day."

Conor chuckled. "Let's go find your sister. My work here is done."

Five

Ellie stood at the kitchen window, drying the same pot she'd been holding for the past ten minutes, and watched her brother and Conor play a restrained game of catch in the backyard. Conor had been back in their lives for a little over a week, and already she noticed a difference in Kirby's outlook. While she was delighted to see her sibling out of the house and showing interest in something other than television, she regarded Conor's intervention with mixed emotions.

With Kirby finally showing signs of moving forward, he would no longer need Ellie as much. At some level it hurt that she hadn't been able to coax him out of his funk. Kirby was her twin, the other half of her heart. She would do anything for him. Even if that meant taking a backseat while once again Kirby and Conor bonded as they had as kids and inadvertently left her out.

Kirby wasn't the only one whose future was a big, daunting blank. Ellie was equally adrift, though perhaps not so visibly. Once Kirby got settled in a hospital where he chose to do his work, and once Ellie's parents returned from the jungle to look after Grandpa, Ellie would no longer be needed.

Except by Emory.

She and her toddler would have to build a new life together. Without Kevin. Where would she start? She couldn't imagine going back to South America with all of her family now in the States, or soon to be. DC had the greatest possibilities for jobs. And she could certainly get good references. But did she want to raise her child inside the Beltway?

Her own childhood had been idyllic here in Silver Glen. A small town with an international flavor thanks to the high-end tourism trade. But the nearest embassy was far, far away. As far as employment went, her skill set was not exactly marketable in the mountains of North Carolina.

As she pondered the murky future, her sunny-natured son sat in his high chair, enthralled with a set of aluminum measuring spoons. She couldn't believe how quickly he was growing. Soon she would have to shop for eighteen-month-sized clothes. Though his birthday was still a ways off, he was big for his age…and tall.

A sudden knock at the back door startled her. Conor poked his head in. "Can you grab us a couple of water bottles, Ellie?"

"Of course." When she handed them over, her fingers brushed his. Conor smelled of hot cotton and male sweat and lime-based aftershave. It was a surprisingly alluring scent.

Conor didn't quite meet her eyes. "Thanks."

Before he could retreat, she put her hand on his arm. "How is he doing, Conor? Really. He tells me he's fine, but clearly he's not."

Conor moved casually, enough that her hand fell away. "He's going to be okay. His head's still messed up. He blames himself for what happened. And he's still conflicted about the job thing. But give him time."

Though Conor was clearly impatient to leave, Ellie powered on, struck by the inescapable notion that she was about to miss something very important in her life if she didn't act.

"Conor..." She trailed off, at a loss for words, feeling the urgency of emotions tangled in her chest.

"Yes?" His body language was one huge rejection. But she was no longer a girl easily swayed.

"I'm glad you're here for Kirby, but *I've* missed you, too. I'm looking forward to the dance at the hotel next week."

He froze, his big frame taut, like an animal sensing danger. "My family will enjoy seeing you again."

"And what about you, Conor?" She put it on the line. No pride. No games. Just the need to *feel* something again other than worry and pain and distress.

He clenched one of the bottles so hard the plastic cracked. Water shot all over the kitchen. "Sorry," he muttered. He grabbed for a roll of paper towels, but she took it out of his hands.

"Leave it," she said. "I'll mop it up in a minute." Again she put a hand on his arm. "Can't we be friends again, too?" she whispered. The muscles in his forearm were hard and warm beneath her fingertips. He was a grown man, utterly masculine, breathtakingly sexy. She looked up at him, letting him see her confused searching, her yearning to feel like a woman again.

For long seconds, their gazes tangled, hers beseeching, his stormy.

At last, he spoke. "I *am* your friend, Ellie. But that's all it can be. I'm the same guy I was a decade ago. You told me way back then I had to choose, and you were right. Now you're grieving and maybe lonely, but those are bad reasons to play with fire."

Before she could respond, he cupped her cheek with his free hand. His fingers were hot against her skin, lightly callused. Firm. Tender. She could swear the air in the small kitchen was charged with electricity. Though several window units cooled the house, her skin was damp.

"I assumed you were also the kind of man who lived for the moment. Has that changed?"

He shrugged, his thumb stroking her cheekbone, perhaps unconsciously. "No. Not really. But even I know better than to get involved with a woman who's lost so much and is still dealing with grief. I'll be here for you, Ellie. For talking and advice and even the occasional platonic outing. But nothing more. You'll thank me later."

"God, you're a patronizing ass," she said, feeling the burn of unshed tears in her throat and her eyes. "I'm a grown woman. I can make my own decisions."

He nodded. "I know that. But maybe I'm going to be the strong one this time. You've spent the last eighteen months taking care of everyone but yourself. You lost your husband. You nearly lost your twin. Your parents live a continent away. Your grandfather is fading before your eyes. You can count on me, Ellie."

"But only as a brother."

"Yeah…"

"I *have* a brother," she said, turning her lips against his palm and kissing him there. "I don't need another." The fact that his pompous speech held elements of truth was something she didn't want to admit.

His groan sounded like a man being tortured. "Don't do this, Ell. Please."

Though it took all she had, she pulled away.

Conor represented an escape from the humdrum difficulties of her everyday life. He was alive and exciting and wonderfully familiar. She wanted to nuzzle into his embrace and never come up for air.

But there was too much history between them. And too much guilt on her part. "Fine," she said, the word as snippy as she could make it. "We're friends. I get it." She bent and began sopping up water.

Conor squatted beside her, forcing her to meet his gaze. "Please don't be mad, Ellie. I couldn't bear it. You and Kirby are very special to me. I'm damned glad you've come home."

He meant it. She could see it in his eyes. "I'm not mad," she said, concealing the depth of her disappointment. She stood and fished another water bottle out of the fridge. "Go play ball. I've got this."

Eight days later she stood in front of the bathroom mirror and second-guessed her wardrobe choice. She had lost most of her baby weight, but her breasts were definitely bigger. The red dress had seemed like a good idea for the holiday-themed soiree, but the just-above-the-knee frock exposed an awful lot of skin. Then again, it *was* August.

The silk fabric clung to her body like a second skin. Not slutty, but in the posh neighborhood next door. A plunging neckline and rhinestone spaghetti straps flattered her shoulders.

She had taken two thick strands of hair at her temples, braided them and twisted them around her crown. The rest of her hair fell straight to her shoulders. It had occurred to her to put all of it up in deference to the heat, but she remembered Conor teasing her about it when they were younger. Always touching her head or tugging a lock.

She wanted him to remember how close they had been. She craved a return to normalcy. Those years and days with Conor were some of the best of her life. A simpler time. An uncomplicated time.

As she walked into the living room, Kirby whistled long and low. "Wow, sis. You look hot."

She blushed. "Thank you. Are you positive you can—"

He interrupted her with an outstretched hand. "Stop right there. I'm a fully trained medical professional. Surely you trust me to take care of one old man and one little baby for one single evening."

"Of course I do, but you've been…"

"I've been dragging you down."

"Don't say that, Kirby. It's not true."

He came over and hugged her, resting his chin on her head. "I love you, Ellie. And I owe you more than I can ever say. I'm sorry it took me so long to get back on my feet."

"Oh, gosh, Kirby. That's a terrible pun."

He laughed along with her. "Sorry. It just came out that way." He held her at arm's length, his gaze locking on hers. "If you ever want to talk about Kevin, I want you to know I'll listen. God knows you've spent enough hours dealing with my tragedies. I'll never forgive myself for being so lost and unavailable when you needed me most."

"Stop," she said, almost in tears. "You nearly *died*, Kirby. Where else was I going to be than with you?"

"And have you let yourself deal with Kevin's death?"

His blunt question caught her off guard. She

sucked in a sharp breath. “I don’t want to talk about that.”

“You never do, hon. That’s the problem. A branch can only bend so far before it breaks. You’ve held everything in for far too long.”

“And now that you’re feeling better, you think you have the right to dig around inside my head?” She was angry with him for ruining her anticipation of the evening.

Kirby’s warm, troubled gaze made her feel far too vulnerable. “If not me, then somebody. We can find a therapist here in Silver Glen. This is important, Ellie. I talked to Mom and Dad recently. They’re worried about you, too. I thought you’d shared things with them, and they thought you were talking to me. But turns out, you haven’t said a damn thing to anyone.”

“Back off, Kirby. I mean it. I’m a grown woman. I know how to take care of myself. If I need help, I’ll ask for it.”

He stared at her for long seconds, making her want to fidget in her high heels. But she held her ground. His shoulders rose and fell. “Okay. It’s your call.”

“Yes, it is.” The subject demanded to be changed.

"Do you have any questions about Emory's routine?"

"I live with you, Ellie. I think I'm pretty familiar with what goes on."

"And dinner?"

"I've already ordered delivery pizza for Grandpa and me. And I'll feed Emory exactly what you want him to have. Have fun, Ellie. Please. And if you don't come home until morning, it will be fine."

Her eyes widened. Hot color flooded from her throat to her hairline. "Why would you say such a thing?"

Kirby eyed her with a gaze that saw straight through to her jumbled emotions. "I'd have to be blind not to see the attraction between you two. I guess it was there way back in high school, but I was too stupid to see it."

"Conor and I are just friends."

"You could do worse when it comes to relationships. He's a good man, Ellie. The best."

She nearly blurted out that she had made her availability perfectly clear and Conor had shut her down. But she didn't want to do anything to cause discord between the two men. Kirby was very protective of his twin sister. If he thought Conor had hurt her, there would be hell to pay.

"Yes, he is," she said quietly. "But I'm only going to be here in Silver Glen until Mom and Dad return to the States. I'm glad Conor is back in our lives. That's as far as it goes."

The ring of the doorbell saved her from further uncomfortable conversation with her meddling brother. In all fairness, she had meddled in his life on a large scale. But that didn't mean she needed or wanted the tables to be turned.

When Kirby walked toward the door, she watched him, happy to see that he was more and more comfortable with his new foot. He had ongoing pain…that, she understood. But what she hoped was that he would get so accustomed to the prosthesis he would forget that his life had been compromised.

Conor entered the room and stopped dead when he saw Ellie. "Wow. You look amazing."

"Thank you," she said primly, wishing Kirby were anywhere else at the moment. "You don't look bad yourself."

That was the understatement of the year. Conor Kavanagh in a tuxedo made the angel choirs sing.

His formal attire had clearly been tailored to fit his tall, lanky body. Broad shoulders, trim hips and long legs added up to one fine-looking specimen of manhood.

Thinking about his *manhood* was a really bad idea. For a woman who hadn't had sex in a year and a half, Conor was the equivalent of a steak dinner with all the trimmings. He was, quite simply, delicious.

She picked up her clutch purse and the cobwebby shawl that was supposed to protect her from any air-conditioned-induced chills. "I'm ready." She turned to her brother. "Promise you'll text me if anything goes wrong."

"It won't, but I will. Have fun, you two."

She kissed his cheek. "I love you, Kirby."

Conor took her elbow as they walked down the front walk toward his fancy European sports car. She knew less than nothing about automobiles, but the sleek, black roadster looked expensive.

When he held the door for her and she slipped into the passenger seat, she was greeted with the smell of warm leather. Oh, Lordy. She was trying *not* to think naughty thoughts, but this car was sex on four wheels.

She paused a moment to consider how many different women Conor might have slept with over the years, but she didn't really want to know. As far as she was concerned, her escort tonight was a grown-up version of the teenage boy she had once known and loved.

"Nice wheels," she quipped when he slid into the driver's seat.

"Thanks. Cars are my weakness. If I hadn't been a skier, I might have ended up being a race car driver."

"The need for speed."

"Something like that..."

She watched him out of the corner of her eye as they drove up the winding mountain road. His hands were confident on the steering wheel, his body relaxed, though he took the curves a little too enthusiastically for her taste.

Conor's assurance stood in direct contrast to her own mixed-up emotions. She was almost a hundred percent sure that tonight's outing had been Kirby's idea. Conor had made it very clear that he and Ellie were not supposed to be anything more than friends. But Kirby was worried about her, so he had probably badgered Conor into extending this invitation.

Even under those circumstances, she was glad to be here.

The trip was far too short for her taste. In no time at all, they arrived at their destination.

The Silver Beeches Lodge was a magnificent building set into the side of the mountain near the very top. It looked out over the valley below with a commanding presence.

When Conor pulled onto the large flagstone apron in front of the hotel, an employee appeared instantly to take the keys and park the car. Conor came around to open Ellie's door and helped her out, one hand on her elbow.

"I have fond memories of this place," she said softly, taking in every feature of the beautiful hotel. "Your mother used to let us do our homework in one of the empty guest rooms. We thought that was so cool."

"She'd be hard-pressed to do that now. There's rarely a vacancy anymore."

Sweeping steps led to imposing doors. Though the hotel was impressive on any given day, tonight it was even more so. Two huge Fraser firs, draped in twinkly lights and iridescent stars, stood like sentinels to greet guests as they arrived.

Conor and Ellie joined the snaking line of people and climbed the stairs. The festive air should have been incongruous given the blazing temperatures, but once inside, it was clear that everyone was prepared to get into the holiday spirit.

A uniformed employee stood in the lobby with a silver bucket, receiving donations for Maeve Kavanagh's favorite charity. Above and across the reception area, a large gold-and-cream banner proclaimed: Christmas in August…'Tis the Season for Giving.

Everywhere, clusters of mistletoe dangled from red velvet ropes, and plaid bows decorated the chandeliers.

Conor took her arm and steered her toward the spot where Maeve Kavanagh held court, welcoming guests and dispensing warmth and cheer. Conor kissed his mother's cheek. "You've got a great crowd," he said. "Congratulations." His mother looked beautiful and confident in a burgundy gown that took ten years off her age.

Maeve nodded. “Thank you, dear. I’m delighted my little event has been received so well.”

Conor urged Ellie forward. “You remember Ellie Porter…right?”

Six

Conor watched his mother sum up his date in one all-encompassing glance. "Of course I do. And Kirby, also. I was so sorry to hear about your brother's accident, Ellie. I hope you'll give him my regards."

"I will, Mrs. Kavanagh. Thank you."

"How is he doing?"

"Better every day. Especially now that he and Conor have reconnected. The two of them are making up for lost time."

Conor could almost see the wheels turning in his mother's brain. She considered it a personal triumph that she had successfully married off four sons. Never mind that all of them were grown men with minds of their own. Maeve liked to think she had a hand in their romances.

Conor decided to nip any Cupid-like ideas in the bud. "Ellie and Kirby are only back in Silver Glen until the late spring. Her parents plan to retire and will be coming home at that time to take care of Mr. Porter. After which Ellie and Kirby will be moving on."

"I see…" Maeve's expression was one-part curiosity and two-parts Machiavellian intent.

"Mother…"

She lifted an eyebrow, trying to look innocent and failing. "What?"

Ellie seemed confused at the byplay. And guests were stacking up behind them waiting to speak to their hostess.

Conor took Ellie's arm. "Let's head on into the ballroom. We'll catch you later, Mom."

As they walked away, Ellie stared up at him with long-lashed eyes. "What was that about?"

"My mother feels the need to meddle in my love life."

"Didn't you tell her that you have no interest at all in me as a potential romantic liaison? That I'm a grieving widow who needs to be protected from her own dangerous impulses? That you're noble and stuffy and totally beyond temptation?"

Taking a detour at the last minute, Conor pulled his date into a narrow hallway and glared at her. "That's not funny."

"I'm not laughing." She took a step toward him, close enough now that he could see the tiny freckle on her right cheek. And the fact that her eyes sparkled with hints of green amidst the blue. She put a hand flat on his chest…right over his heart. "You're a gorgeous, sexy, wonderful man, Conor Kavanagh. The boy I remember has turned into a pretty special human being. I'm happy to be with you tonight."

Without warning, she went up on tiptoe and kissed him smack on the mouth. Somehow, his hands were around her waist and he was kissing her back. So many emotions. So many nuances.

He recognized the sexual need, a healthy man's response to having an attractive woman near. He also acknowledged the sweet sensation of holding his teenage fantasy in his arms. But what was more alarming was the sense of homecoming. Of rightness. As if every woman he'd ever known had simply been a placeholder…marking time until the real thing showed up.

The intense, unexpected feelings scared the crap out of him. He wasn't going to change for any woman. He released her and stepped back, breathing harshly. "I told you this wasn't going to happen."

Ellie crossed her arms beneath her breasts, lifting them into mouthwatering prominence, though he was sure she didn't realize it. "You're not the boss of me, Conor. We aren't kids. And I don't have to take orders from you. I've been running my own life just fine."

"Quit flirting with me," he demanded, already undressing her in his head. Two things held him back. First, the knowledge of her dead husband. A year and a half wasn't long enough to work through that kind of grief. And secondly, the memory of how a younger Ellie had judged him and found him wanting.

"Fine," she said. "You're my other brother. I get the message. Can we go to the party now?"

She turned her back on him and headed for the ballroom, leaving him to trail in her wake. He was accustomed to being in control of his life. Of charting his own course. But Ellie challenged his preconceptions of her at every turn.

The view from the back didn't help his resolve. Her long tanned legs and narrow waist showcased a curvy bottom. That red dress had been created by some designer to drive a man insane.

So far, it was working.

He had assumed the ballroom would be neutral territory. Too many people to make any rash decisions based on creamy shoulders and a feminine smile that made him ache.

Ellie's face lit up when she heard the band. "Oh, this is wonderful," she said. "I love this song."

It was a Bing Crosby classic about dreaming and Christmas and yearning for the past. Unfortunately for Conor, it was also a slow dance. He took Ellie in his arms with a sense of fatalism. She fit against him perfectly. Her light perfume teased his nose. But it was the slide of her hair against his hand that did him in. Silky. Thick. Like warm cider on a cold night.

It was a really bad idea to bring Ellie this evening. Too much romance in the air. Too many echoes of auld lang syne.

What did she want from him? If they had talked

about Kevin before now, Conor might be more inclined to open up to her. But the fact that her dead husband was carefully sectioned off in a place labeled No Trespassing told him that Ellie had a long way to go before she would be ready to love again. Love didn't die in a mountain-climbing accident.

Maybe she was secretly furious with her husband for risking his life. And maybe that anger was manifesting itself in a flirtation with Conor.

He didn't like being used any more than the next man, but it was going to be difficult to say no, even if he really wanted to. Which he didn't.

Ellie Porter pushed all his buttons. She always had. Which meant that Conor was in a hell of a predicament.

The Bing song ended and another crooner took center stage, again singing a slow, haunting melody. Conor and Ellie hadn't exchanged a single word since he took her in his arms. If he were a whimsical man, he'd have said they were bound together by the magic of the past…by the years of playing together, studying together, growing up together.

They had so many shared experiences, so much

in common when it came to their roots. But beyond that was an entire decade when they'd been on opposite sides of the equator...when life had taken them in each on radically different paths.

Ellie made a small noise, and he pulled back, incredulous. "Are you crying?" he asked, aghast.

"Of course not." She frowned at him, but her cheeks were damp.

Before Conor could deal with that information, the first of his brothers cut in. It was a half hour or more before he had a chance to dance with his date again. First came Liam and Dylan. They both remembered Ellie in passing. But they were older and not as familiar with her as Aidan and Gavin, who were closer in school.

Patrick, sixth in the lineup of Kavanagh brothers, also took a turn around the dance floor with Ellie. Only James, the youngest, was not in attendance tonight.

By the time Conor reclaimed Ellie, she professed herself tired and ready to hit the buffet. "I'm starving," she said. Her cheeks were flushed with color and her eyes sparkled. "That was so much fun. Your brothers are wonderful."

While Ellie was occupied with the Kavanagh

men, Conor had passed the time by dancing with his sisters-in-law, each of whom was very dear to him. Zoe and Mia. Emma and Cassidy. The new additions to the Kavanagh clan were smart, sexy, beautiful women. His brothers were damn lucky.

It irked him that dancing with his siblings had made Ellie happy, while Conor's greatest achievement was to make her cry. But he kept his disgruntlement to himself.

Over hors d'oeuvres and wine, he studied Ellie when he thought she wasn't watching. Though she smiled and spoke to a number of people who remembered the Porter family, there was an aura of sadness around her. Conor wondered if he was the only person who noticed.

He sensed in her a fatigue that was more than physical. Perhaps he was seeing evidence of the mental toll she had endured. Some people in her shoes might have experienced a total breakdown. After months of worry and grief and unrelenting work, it was understandable if Ellie was fragile emotionally. And yet, she impressed him as one of the strongest women he had ever known.

He stole a large boiled shrimp from her plate and dipped it in cocktail sauce. "So tell me about life in the jungle," he said. "It must have been strange and exotic at the same time. Did you eat the local food? Speak the lingo?" Keeping the conversation light and impersonal was his way of coping with the evening.

Ellie nodded, licking a crumb from her lower lip. "Oh, yes. Aside from the fact that provisions were hard to come by, Mom and Dad wanted us to acclimate to the local culture. We became fluent in Spanish and Quechua. We learned how to build a hut out of banana leaves. We knew exactly which insects were harmless and which ones could kill us."

"I'm impressed. Maybe I should start calling you Jane of the Jungle."

"Does that mean you can picture me in a leopard-print bikini?" She swallowed a sip of wine and stared him down.

His temper fired along with his libido. "I'm trying damned hard to be a gentleman, Ellie. You're hurting. I get that. But having a fling with me is only going to make you feel worse."

She stared at him, spine erect, chin tilted upward the tiniest bit. "It must be lovely to be omniscient.

Do you and God triage the world's problems every morning?"

"You're a piece of work, do you know that?"

She shrugged. "My husband is gone, Conor. I'm pretty clear about that. And *I'll* be gone from Silver Glen in no time at all. I have a baby who will never know his father and a brother who's struggling as much as I am. Is it so wrong for me to want you?"

Conor felt helpless and confused. The last time he'd felt this level of anxiety was in the aftermath of his horrific accident. Even now he could remember the moment he heard a dreadful pop in his knee and ended up facedown in the snow with one leg bent at an inhuman angle.

Surviving that moment in his life had been no small achievement. He'd hung on, because the alternative had been unthinkable. And he'd known he was right to let Ellie go, because he was not able to change the basic core of who he was. For years as a kid he'd watched his mother try to keep tabs on her gadabout husband.

The end of that struggle had meant heartbreak for everyone. Conor had learned a valuable lesson. He had to be who he was.

Now, here with Ellie, he felt a similar torture. Did he want her? Hell yes. But he couldn't get past the fact that she was acting out of desperation. He owed it to her to be the smart one this time. To make wise decisions.

He took one of her hands in his, not caring that they might have witnesses. "Will you tell me about Kevin?" he asked softly, trying in every way he knew how to communicate his compassion and his concern for her.

Ellie jerked free and wiped her hands on a snowy linen napkin. "No," she said. "I won't. This is a *Christmas* party, Conor. Your timing leaves a lot to be desired."

"It's August, not December. And you're putting a wall between us. I don't like it."

"Is that a requirement? You have to like everything I do?"

She was stubborn and angry and totally adorable. He chose his words carefully. "Maybe it's petty of me, but I'm not crazy about the idea of standing in for a dead man."

The shock on her face was almost instantly replaced by another expression. He saw in that moment she had never considered the possibility his mind might go in another direction.

She swallowed hard. Her hand trembled when she carefully pushed her plate aside. They were seated at a table in an out-of-the-way corner. It was doubtful they could be overheard. But she lowered her voice and leaned forward. "I'm embarrassed, Conor, that you would even think that. If we end up in bed together, I'll know exactly who I'm with. I'm lonely and sad and it's been so long since I've been touched sexually that I probably won't remember what to do, but I'll *know* you. It's you I want."

"Why?" he asked bluntly.

She shook her head, her eyes bleak. "I'm a single mom. I have no desire to go out and cruise bars. The chance of any man wanting to marry me knowing it's a package deal with Emory is slim. But I'm young and healthy and I have needs like any other woman. You're very special to me. I care about you. And I trust you. I think being with you in that way would be…well…"

She stumbled to a halt, the color in her cheeks rivaling her dress.

Conor bowed his head. When he finally looked

up at her, he caught a flicker in her eyes that made his heart race. “Are you sure, Ellie? I don’t want to hurt you. Things ended badly between us the last time.”

This time it was *her* small hand that closed on his bigger one. Though her touch was light, he felt it all the way to his gut. His sex stirred even as his breath hitched in his chest.

“I’m sure, Conor. Very sure. But if you’re not, we won’t take this any further.” She glanced around the room, restlessness in her body language. “Why don’t we dance again?”

It seemed like a good idea. A socially acceptable way for him to be close to her while he sorted through the pitfalls he could see in front of them.

The room was crowded and loud. Despite what the calendar said, a holiday air permeated the assembly. The massive fireplaces at either end of the large salon were filled with pots of foil-wrapped poinsettias instead of roaring flames. Conor hadn’t the slightest idea how his mother had managed to pull that off in the midst of summer.

Everyone seemed to be dancing—young and old…talented and awkward. Maeve Kavanagh had always possessed the gift of hospitality. Whether she threw a kid's birthday or a fancy affair, it was guaranteed to be a success.

The crush of partygoers made it necessary for Conor to hold Ellie close or risk having someone step on her. If he closed his eyes, this might have been many years ago. Kirby and Ellie had often attended special occasions at Silver Beeches. The first time Conor had ever danced with her, he had been fourteen years old. Having a girl in his arms, any girl, would have been plenty of stimulation for an adolescent boy. But since the girl was Ellie, well…he could be excused for fantasizing about that night for weeks to come.

And now here they were.

For a lot of men, this would be the perfect setup. Two adults indulging in a mutually satisfying sexual relationship. No expectations. No strings. No future. Conor had participated in a few such liaisons over the years. And never with repercussions.

But Ellie came with a whole laundry list of repercussions. Kirby's reaction, for one. For the first time in over a decade, Conor had his old friends back in his life. And it was pretty damn great.

What would happen to their triangle if Conor took Ellie to his bed?

Then there was little Emory. Ellie needed to be on the lookout for a man who wanted an instant family…a man who would look forward to coaching Little League and shepherding Boy Scouts. Conor knew next to nothing about babies. He was learning from the additions to his brothers' families, but that didn't mean he was a fit parent.

In the end, though, his approach to life was what took him out of the running. Shouldn't Ellie wait for *the one*? Having sex with Conor would only postpone her chances to rebuild a life for her and her son.

Ellie rested her head on his shoulder, disarming him completely. All of his mental gyrations were nothing more than a smokescreen easily blown away. If Ellie wanted to be wild and irresponsible, was he really going to stop her?

She felt right in his arms, despite what his brain told him. He *needed* to have this time with her, even if he was still the same kind of man she hadn't wanted in the past.

Ellie curled a hand behind his shoulder and touched the place where his hair met his neck.

His barber had done a good job. "I can almost hear you thinking," she said. "Chill out. Relax. It's Christmas." Her fingertips on his skin were like fire.

He laughed, but he wasn't really amused. It was easy to pretend for one night. Christmas was about dreams and special wishes and sharing love.

But tonight wasn't December 25, and he and Ellie weren't talking about love. That was something she had shared with her husband, marked by a wedding ring and vows. *'Til death do us part.* Never had that phrase seemed so starkly real.

What she wanted from Conor was far less cerebral. He had never been in love. The closest he had ever come was his adolescent crush on Ellie. But even he knew that such a juvenile emotion was only a pale imitation of what Ellie and Kevin must have shared.

The song ended, and part of the crowd began to drift toward the exits. Four hours had flown by though Conor had scarcely noticed. He glanced at his watch. "I should get you home," he said gruffly.

Ellie took his hand in hers, the simple gesture making his resolve crumble. “Yours first,” she said.

He halted in the midst of the exodus, the throng of guests parting on either side of him to continue on their way. “What do you mean?”

“Take me home, Conor. To your house. I’ve never seen it. Wouldn’t you like to give me a tour?”

Seven

Ellie had never thrown herself at a man so blatantly. If Conor didn't crack this time, she was going to back off. A girl had to have some pride, after all. "Come on," she said. "People are staring at us."

They said their goodbyes to Maeve, but the moment was brief, because Conor's mother was mobbed by well-wishers encouraging her to keep up the Christmas in August tradition every year. By the time Conor and Ellie made it outside, it was dark, the moonless night stuffy and warm.

Perhaps because Conor was the owner's son, a valet brought the car around to the side of the hotel so they wouldn't have to wait forever. There were definitely perks to being a Kavanagh. Even so, the line of traffic to exit the hotel driveway was slow moving.

Once they were in the car, Ellie felt totally alone. A silent Conor drummed his fingers on the steering wheel, his face in shadowy profile beneath the exterior lights of the hotel. He looked anything but happy.

"Take me home," she said abruptly. "It's late. I'm exhausted." And she was tired of battling Conor's scruples and misgivings.

Clearly he wasn't as interested in her as she thought. Or else he wouldn't be clinging so vehemently to his notion that the two of them shouldn't end up naked together.

"Make up your mind, Ellie." His grumpy response infuriated her.

Suddenly, she lost it. For months she had told herself life would get back to normal. She'd forced herself to believe it, even if the pleasant fiction was only a ruse to get from one day to the next. Seeing Conor again had been the first hint of happiness she had experienced since Kevin died.

But Conor didn't want her. Heartsick and humiliated, she threw open the door of the car, stepped out and slammed the fancy piece of metal. "I'll get a ride with someone else," she said, her tone as snarky as she could make it. She heard him yell at her, but she didn't stop.

She walked quickly into the dark night, circling around the hotel and disappearing into the gardens on the far side. Pausing only long enough to slip off her high heels, she moved forward blindly and quickly, trying to outrun the pain. Tiny pieces of gravel lacerated her feet.

She kept on. The neatly manicured gardens eventually gave way to a familiar rough path that led to a waterfall. The going was more difficult here. Roots and stones were silent adversaries in the inky gloom. Her lungs burned. Her chest heaved. Her throat was raw.

Sweat rolled down her back. Her beautiful dress was going to be ruined. She knew it and she didn't care. Nothing mattered. Nothing made sense. Behind her she thought she caught the sound of Conor's voice. Yelling. Demanding.

She ignored him. In some dim corner of her brain she remembered that the trail ended at the waterfall. What would she do then? Throw herself in? She had a son. That wasn't an option. Pain rose up inside her like a writhing beast.

Without warning, an unseen obstacle caught her toe and sent her crashing to the ground. All the wind left her lungs and the world went black as searing pain spread from her temple into nothingness…

Conor should have been able to catch Ellie easily. His long legs could far outstrip her stride. But he'd had to waste precious seconds easing the car out of the way so he wouldn't block the hotel drive.

By the time he bounded after her, she had disappeared.

He knew she wouldn't go inside the hotel…not in her condition. The only other viable option was the hotel garden. There he found her shoes. Tucking them in his jacket pockets, he loped after her, sure now that she was headed down the trail she and Conor and Kirby had traversed often as kids.

His heart jerked erratically in his chest as he ran. It was dark. The path was rough and dangerous in these conditions.

When he heard her cry out sharply, his blood congealed. Dear God. What had she done to herself?

He found her crumpled and still in the middle of the trail. In fact, he almost tripped over her. For several sick, stunned moments, he thought she was dead. But when he took her limp wrist in his hand, he found a steady pulse.

Should he move her? Had she broken anything? Breathing harshly, he grabbed his phone from his pocket and activated the flashlight app. Carefully easing her head to one side, he looked for damage. And found it. Blood oozed from a deep gash on her forehead.

Hell… His first-aid training kicked in and he began moving his hands over her limbs methodically. Everything seemed okay, but it was impossible to be sure.

He shook her gently. “Ellie. Ellie. Wake up, sweetheart. Talk to me.”

The next minute and a half stretched into a lifetime, but finally she stirred. “Conor?” The word was slurred.

“Yes, love. I’m here.” He pointed the beam of light away from her face so it wouldn’t blind her.

She struggled to sit up. He helped her, though fear lingered that she might be badly hurt. “Where’s Kirby?” she asked.

The odd question caught him off guard. “Um… at home.”

“Oh.” She put a hand to her head. “Why is my face wet?”

“You cut yourself when you fell. And you were crying.”

Her chin wobbled. “I know. Because Kirby and I have to leave.”

“You do?”

“We tried, Conor, I swear. But Mom and Dad won’t budge. They’re making us go with them to South America.” She burst into tears.

Conor crouched beside her, stunned and more scared than he had been in a very long time. Something had happened. Something bad. And he had to get help. Fast.

Taking off his jacket, he wrapped it around Ellie. Her skin was ice-cold, she might be going into shock. Even though she had spoken to him, now she seemed to be drifting in and out of consciousness.

Taking a few steps away from her, he made two

hurried phone calls…one to his brother Gavin and one to Kirby. Gavin and Cassidy agreed to head straight to the Porters' house to look after the baby and Mr. Porter. As soon as they arrived, Kirby would leave to meet Conor at the hospital.

Even though Conor was speaking in a low voice, Ellie should have been able to hear what he was saying. She should have demanded to know why he was calling her brother. Or why he was contacting Gavin. But she did neither.

With the plan set into motion, Conor knelt and scooped her into his arms. Her head lolled against his shoulder.

"Ellie," he said urgently as he stood and began rapidly retracing their steps. He wanted to run, but he couldn't risk dropping her or falling himself. She seemed so small suddenly…and fragile. God, what was wrong with her? A concussion?

The trail was not more than half a mile in length, but it seemed endless. He didn't waste time calling for an ambulance. He could get Ellie to the hospital more quickly, especially since the traffic from the party had now dissipated.

At his car, he set her gently in the passenger

seat, reclined it and belted her in. "Ellie, honey. Can you open your eyes?"

She did as he asked, but though she smiled weakly, her gaze was unfocused and her eyelids fluttered shut again.

He knew in detail how to ski downhill at breakneck speeds, making the most of every curve and straight stretch. He'd been known to do the same in a car heading up and down this mountain. But now he was torn between speed and caution.

The trip became a blur. He drove automatically, his gaze flitting every five seconds to his passenger. Second-guessing himself again and again, he cursed beneath his breath. Maybe he should have waited for the ambulance.

Fortunately, Kirby had been cleared for driving since his right foot was intact. He sent half-a-dozen texts that Conor was not able to read until he hit a traffic light in town. Kirby was frantic. And he would be at least twenty minutes behind Conor.

The hospital emergency room was top-notch. The Kavanagh family had made numerous large gifts over the years. Plus, Conor and his brothers had kept them in business with various injuries.

Broken arms. Sprained ankles. And, of course, Conor's torn-up knee.

When the admitting nurse passed them off to a physician, Conor spoke rapidly as the man assessed Ellie's condition. "I'd like to call in Dr. Milledge for a consult, if you don't mind. He's a family friend."

The ER doctor nodded. "No problem. I wouldn't mind a second opinion about this head injury. Tell me again what she said?"

"When I found her, she had tripped and fallen. There was a rock with blood on it, so that explains the cut. But when she opened her eyes and spoke to me, she didn't seem to be in the present."

"Got it." The doctor tucked a chart under his arm. "We'll call Dr. Milledge, but in the meantime, we'll see what we can find out. Are you her next of kin?"

"No. That would be her brother, Kirby Porter. But he'll be here shortly."

Conor watched helplessly as Ellie was rolled away down the hall on a gurney. Guilt choked him. He'd known she was in trouble…he'd known it in his gut. And yet still he had let her down.

The waiting room was like all hospital waiting rooms. Filled with fear and stale body odor and people with anxious faces. Only in this case, the furnishings and the reading material were upscale. Silver Glen catered not only to locals, but also to well-heeled visitors who often showed their appreciation of top-notch medical care by leaving large donations. Only last fall, an extremely famous pop sensation came down with the flu while spending a few weeks on hiatus. She was so happy with how she was treated that she had her accountant electronically transfer a six-figure gift to the hospital before she left town.

Conor was sitting, head bowed, elbows on his knees, when Kirby appeared at his side. The other man sat down and ran a hand over his face. “Give me an update.”

“I’ve requested they call in Dr. Milledge. He’s an expert on neurological stuff. I don’t want them to miss anything.”

“What in the hell happened?”

Conor swallowed. No matter how he told this story, he would cast himself in a bad light. But Kirby deserved the truth. “We argued,” he said, his throat tight with regret.

Kirby’s gaze sharpened. “About what?”

Conor stared at him, wondering how he could explain this delicately. "Well, I—"

"Oh, for God's sake, Conor. You're scaring the crap out of me. What the hell happened?"

Conor shrugged helplessly as the weight of his own fear and panic engulfed him. "Ellie wanted intimacy. Physical intimacy. I put her off, thinking she needed to deal with her husband's death before we acted on the attraction we both felt. Ellie got mad and ran away from me."

"Where?"

"The trail to the waterfall. It was dark. She tripped and fell and hit her head on a rock. But honest to God, Kirby, the cut doesn't look all that bad. She may need a few stitches."

"Who knows what else she might have damaged..." Kirby paused, his gaze locked on the far wall as if his physician's brain were assessing all the scenarios. "Tell me more about what she said."

"I roused her. Asked her to speak to me. She wanted to know why her face was wet. When I told her she had been crying, she nodded and said she was upset because your parents were making both of you go to South America."

Kirby paled. "Holy hell."

"Yeah." Conor was still hoping he had misunderstood her.

"As much as I don't want to say this, Ellie might have finally snapped. Not permanently. But maybe in a very bad way. Damn, Conor."

"I blame myself." The words felt like glass in his throat. "She told me she needed to feel that physical connection again. To be held and touched as a woman. God, Kirby, she opened herself up to me and I told her it was a bad idea."

The hole in his chest grew larger by the minute. What had he done?

He dug the heels of his hands into his gritty eyes and waited for Kirby to lambast him. But when he finally looked at his friend, all he could see in Kirby's eyes was pain mixed with sympathy.

Kirby took a deep breath and let it out, absently massaging the leg that was missing a foot. "You were trying to do the right thing, Conor. Most men would have taken advantage of her vulnerability. But you care about her. Of all the people in her life, you're the first person she's reached out to…the first person she's been comfortable enough with to admit she's hurting."

"And I bobbled it." He jumped to his feet, feeling as if the walls were closing in on him. "I assume Gavin and Cassidy got to your house okay?"

"Yes. Grandpa and Emory are already asleep, so they shouldn't have any trouble."

"And Gavin and Cassidy's twins?"

"Mia and Dylan are keeping them at their house overnight.

Conor made a circuit of the small room, pausing to stare out into the darkness. A few hours ago he'd been dancing with Ellie, holding her close, feeling the pulsing current of need that made him hungry to taste her, to find release inside her beautiful body.

Ellie was everything he wanted in a woman. But he would forgo any chance of ever seeing her again if the Fates would let her be okay. Ellie didn't deserve anything that had happened to her. She had a big heart and a generous spirit. She was a steadfast sister, a dutiful daughter and granddaughter, a devoted mom.

He leaned his forehead against the glass…praying. After his accident in high school, he had prayed a lot. But those had been the selfish prayers of a teenage boy. He'd asked God to let him be whole again. To have the chance to be the best in the world at what he did.

How shallow he'd been in his tunnel vision. How little he had known of real life...of the things that mattered deeply. He had a lot to learn from Kirby and Ellie about dealing with tragedy.

Ellie had wanted Conor to help Kirby...to prove to him that there would be a good life after his amputation. But from where Conor was standing, the lessons were all coming *his* way. Ellie's selflessness. Kirby's bravery. The Porter twins had taught him a lot in a very short time.

At last, Dr. Milledge appeared and escorted Kirby and Conor to a nearby family room set up for private conversations.

Conor's heart was beating so fast he felt sick. One quick glance at Kirby's face told him his buddy felt the same.

Dr. Milledge took the lead, his expression composed as he addressed his comments to Kirby. "Your sister is going to be fine. But she's momentarily confused. Not uncommon under these circumstances. Can you fill me in on what might have triggered this?"

Kirby blinked, his jaw working as he fought

to absorb the information. "She lost her husband eighteen months ago in the same accident that nearly killed me. Ellie and I are twins. At the time I was fighting for my life, she found out she was pregnant. She's spent every waking hour caring for me and worrying about me, even as her child was being born."

Dr. Milledge nodded. "Certainly enough trauma to trigger an episode, particularly if she has never processed the grief."

"She hasn't," Conor said. "We had an argument about that very topic tonight. She became very angry with me. Ran away into the woods. And, well…you know the rest."

Kirby interrupted. "And the head wound?"

"She does have a significant concussion. Which likely was catalyst for this episode. We'll do X-rays and CT scans to make sure we aren't over-looking a skull fracture. But I don't think she's in any danger. We'd like to keep her overnight for observation."

"I'll take her to my house when the time comes," Conor said, his protective instincts in high gear.

Kirby frowned. "I'm a doctor. Why wouldn't she simply go home?"

Conor shook his head. “You’ll have your hands full caring for your grandfather. Ellie knows me and trusts me. The ski resort is closed. There’s no reason I can’t give her my full attention.”

Eight

The next afternoon, Conor and Kirby stood outside the hospital waiting for Ellie to be brought outside in a wheelchair.

"Standard operating procedure," Kirby muttered as a uniformed attendant came in sight with precious cargo.

Conor took a step forward, but Ellie never looked at him. Her eyes were glued on Emory, who wriggled in Kirby's arms.

Her face lit up, but her eyes brimmed with tears. "My sweetheart," she cried. "I'm so sorry. Mommy has missed you."

As Ellie stood, Kirby handed over the baby.

Ellie cuddled Emory and smothered his head with kisses.

Ellie had responded well to rest and medication. She understood that she had sustained a head injury and that she had been concussed and temporarily confused.

Now was the tricky part. Kirby put his arm around her. "The doctors say you need to take it easy, sis. I have my hands full taking care of Grandpa, but Conor has arranged for you and Emory to spend a few weeks with him."

A hushed moment of silence fell. Kirby and Conor held their collective breaths. At last, Ellie acknowledged Conor with a small smile. "That would be nice. Thank you, Conor."

He'd been half-afraid he would see anger on her face…or stony dismissal. Hearing her agree to the plan eased part of the weight on his shoulders. "The car seat is in my car," Conor said. "Kirby will follow us up the mountain and help us get settled in."

Before Conor could make a move to put Ellie in the car, she took Emory, tucked him in his seat and slid in beside him, leaving Conor to play chauffeur. Over the roof of the vehicle, Conor looked at Kirby with a lift of his shoulders and a shake of his head. One step at a time.

Conor drove up the mountain with one eye on the rearview mirror and the backseat. It wasn't so much that Ellie ignored him but that she focused every scrap of her attention on the baby. Little Emory was blissfully happy to have his mother back.

Once they arrived at their destination, Conor decided to let Ellie move at her own pace. He grabbed the small bag Kirby had packed for her to have at the hospital. The three adults mounted the steps, Kirby following along behind. He was striding more naturally every day, and he seemed more at peace with his life. For Conor, it was a two-way street. He had missed his old friend, and having Kirby back in his life was a shot in the arm. Kirby would be leaving in the spring, so Conor was determined to enjoy the time they had.

And then there was Ellie. He watched her closely to see how she would react to his home. The house still smelled new. In fact, he had only completed the last bits six months ago. Building this structure had been a labor of love. He was much farther out of town than any of his siblings. But he relished the solitude.

Though his mother had gifted each of her sons with acreage on the mountain between the Silver Beeches Lodge and the ski resort, Conor had taken some of his own savings and bought property on the south end of the mountain. The terrain was rougher here, the sense of privacy more pronounced.

Ellie paused on the wide wraparound porch and smiled. “This is beautiful, Conor. I had no idea you had a house of your own.”

“Well, I lived in an apartment in town for a while…and then a condo. But I suppose I finally grew up and decided I wanted to put down roots. I had lots of help with the architecture and the decorating. But I’m pretty happy with how it turned out.”

All of Silver Glen conspired to maintain an Alpine theme in the picturesque town. The area was known for its atmosphere and its charm. Conor agreed wholeheartedly, but he’d always been drawn to Western design. He’d made several trips to Wyoming and Montana where he had procured large logs from abandoned buildings for the outer shell of his home.

His large porch and the floors inside were constructed of wide oak planking. But there was nothing rough or rustic about the place. He planned to live here for a very long time, so he had paid attention to comfort and luxury and, in some cases, outright decadence. He was deeply moved to know that Ellie and Emory would be his first guests.

In the living room, the three adults paused, no one quite at ease. Kirby spoke first. “I won’t linger. I don’t want to leave Grandpa for too long. Conor has given you and Emory a suite with a bedroom, bathroom and sitting room. Emory won’t be right beside you every night like he was at Grandpa’s house. You’ll sleep better, I’m sure.”

Conor nodded. “Make yourself at home. Take the tour.”

“But what about all of our things? Mine and Emory’s?”

Her brother grinned. “I packed it all up and brought it here yesterday. Turns out, I’m not quite as broken as I thought I was…and you aren’t, either, Ellie. This is only a bump in the road. You took care of me night and day for months. I need the chance to return the favor and to show you I'm as good as new."

Conor was ready for Kirby to go. He wanted to be alone with Ellie. The knowledge that she would be sleeping beneath his roof made his pulse jump and his breathing ragged.

When the door closed behind Kirby, Conor hesitated. "How about some tea?" he asked with forced cheerfulness.

"I think Emory's ready for his nap. Will you show me where I can put him down?"

The baby was indeed yawning. "Of course. Right this way."

Conor stood to one side and watched as Ellie toured the quarters he'd given her. It had been important to him to add some finishing touches in the past twenty-four hours. Fresh flowers. A cashmere throw on the end of the king-size bed. A whimsical pair of bedroom slippers that resembled baby rabbits.

The rooms were done in shades of cream and pale green. With the large windows bringing the outdoors inside, this guest suite reminded him of a springtime forest.

Ellie tucked Emory in the brand-new crib Conor had bought and covered him with a light blanket. The house was air-conditioned comfortably, but the baby's arms and legs were bare.

Emory scarcely stirred as the two adults tiptoed out. To Conor's surprise, Ellie perched on the corner of her own bed and motioned him into a chair. "I'd like to say something," she said quietly.

He sat down and leaned back, trying to feign relaxation, but his gut was tight. "You have the floor," he teased, trying for a light tone.

But Ellie's expression was serious. "Dr. Milledge told me that you and I argued right before my accident."

"That's true."

"Conor…" She trailed off, her hands twisting restlessly in her lap. Today she was dressed simply in nice jeans and a white knit shirt with short sleeves. Her beautiful hair was caught up in a ponytail. The style drew attention to her high cheekbones and slightly pointed chin.

He waited, remembering the doctor's advice. *No pressure.* "Nothing to worry about, Ellie. You and I are fine."

"I'm sorry," she said, eyes downcast. "It was

probably my fault. That's the thing that's bugging me. I can't remember."

She looked up at him, and he saw panic in her eyes.

Without overthinking it, he joined her on the bed. Hip to hip, but not touching. "It was nothing, Ellie. Really."

"I remember the party and the hospital, but in between is a blank."

He put his arm around her shoulders and drew her close against his side, unable to resist the need to comfort her. "According to the doctors, that's entirely normal for a head injury. Those brief hours may come back or they may not, but either way, it's no big deal."

She sighed, her expression hidden as she pressed her cheek to his chest. "It is to me," she said. "Please, Conor, tell me what we were fighting about."

Well, hell. What was he supposed to say? "It was more of a disagreement."

"I was running through the forest barefoot. It had to be something." One second passed. Then five.

Searching for a believable lie was not easy.

Ellie pulled free of his embrace and turned sideways so she could look up at him, her blue eyes allowing him no quarter. “You can tell me. I’m not going to shatter into a million pieces. What did we argue about, Conor?”

He cleared his throat. “Well…”

“Was it about sex?”

He felt his neck heat. “Why would you say that?”

“I’m attracted to you. And I think you are to me. So it seems like the topic might have come up. But I don’t know why it would be the kind of thing to make me so upset.”

He cupped a hand behind her neck, steadying her…steadying himself…willing her to understand. “You wanted us to be intimate. I wanted that, too. But I was afraid it was too soon…that you hadn’t dealt with Kevin’s death.”

She went white…so pale he thought for a moment she might faint. And he felt her tremble. “It must be nice to be right all the time.”

While he struggled for the right words to say, Ellie stood up and went to the window, her back to him. “I’d like to take a nap now,” she said. “If that’s okay.”

The dismissal was pretty clear. “Of course.”

He didn’t want to leave her, but he had no real reason to stay.

The house seemed to close in on him suddenly, and he wondered what in the heck he had done to himself. Ellie was already upset with him, and they hadn’t even made it through the first day. Had he sentenced himself to an interminably long few weeks?

For half an hour Conor settled himself in front of the muted TV with a beer and his laptop to deal with a few things at Silver Slopes. But none of the business was really urgent. Not to mention the fact that he had an accountant and a host of other employees to handle anything that might come up.

Finally, he realized that he had to do something physical to diffuse the restless energy that thrummed through his veins. He wanted Ellie badly. And she was ensconced in his home. Close. Available. It was enough to drive him stark raving mad.

Surmising that Ellie and Emory would sleep at least an hour and a half, he went to his bedroom, stripped down to his boxers and donned a T-shirt and shorts. At the back of his new home he had added a state-of-the-art workout gym.

In minutes, he was sweating as he pummeled a punching bag. His knuckles would be sore and bruised tomorrow, but it was worth it. After that, he moved to the weight bench. Adding five pounds to his personal best, he lay down on his back, positioned his hands and concentrated fiercely as his arms strained to lift the almost immovable object.

Salty perspiration dripped into his eyes, making them sting and burn. His lungs ached for air, and his biceps quivered with fatigue.

The sudden sound of a woman's voice almost made him drop the weights. Gritting his teeth, he lowered the bar into its resting place. Taking a deep breath, he sat up and wiped his face with a towel. "I thought you were sleeping."

Ellie's curious stare made him restless. "I'm a good power napper." She crossed the room to stand beside him. "You're a very masculine man, Conor Kavanagh. I like looking at you." As sweat rolled down his shoulder, she ran her fingertip from the inside of his elbow up his arm and caught the droplet.

Her touch on his body burned him from the inside out. “I need a shower,” he muttered, scarcely able to breathe. Arousal bloomed, hot and vicious. Surely Ellie wasn’t this naive. “Will you excuse me?”

As he started to step around her, she placed a hand, palm flat, on his bare chest. He had stripped off his T-shirt before doing the weights. “No,” she said. “I don’t believe I will.”

“Stop, Ellie.” As a protest, it was weak at best. But the last time he’d rejected her she had ended up with a concussion and memory loss.

“I’ve had professional medical care, Conor. You don’t have to be afraid you’re going to shatter my psyche. If you don’t want me, you can say so.”

He could make her back off. All he had to do was convince her that he looked at her as a sister. Sadly, it would take a hell of a better man than he was to sell that lie.

He curled his fingers around her wrist, removing her hand from his chest. “I’ll give you whatever you want, Ellie, I swear. But we have to start slowly.”

She nodded, still with that curious light in her eyes…as if she were already imagining the two of them naked and entwined in the sheets. "That's fair. So a kiss, then?"

She made it a question even as she moved against him, heedless of his damp nakedness. Lifting her face to his, she put her hand on the back of his head. "Kiss me."

A very long time ago he had danced with her and wondered how it would be to kiss a girl like Ellie. But this was different. In the interim, she'd been married…had given birth to a child. Conor was not into one-night stands, though he'd had his share of relationships.

Slowly, he lowered his mouth to hers. He'd never really thought of her as a short woman, but they were both barefoot and Ellie seemed small and vulnerable. That vulnerability gave him pause. Should he walk away from temptation?

When his lips touched hers, the internal discussion ended. His brain shut down instantly and his body took over. God, she felt amazing. His hands roved over her back. He badly wanted to feel her curvy butt in his palms, but protecting her had to come before his own base urges. He had to keep a tight rein on his hunger or it would consume them both.

"Ellie," he muttered. "Ah, God, Ellie."

Her arms went around his neck. "Hold me, Conor." Her voice broke. "I need you so much."

The need went both ways. He'd always assumed what he felt for one of his two best friends was a crush. Puppy love. The infatuation of a hormonal teenage boy for a beautiful girl. But what if it had been more? What if that emotion had lain dormant all these years? What if every woman he'd met had been judged by the yardstick that was Ellie?

Her lips were soft and sweet. At first, the kiss was chaste. He wasn't willing to torment either of them with a prelude that had no second act. In moments, though, her restrained enthusiasm sparked a naughty demon in his gut. A devil's advocate that said he would cherish her in bed. Make her feel like a queen. A goddess. Where was the harm in that?

When Ellie parted her lips, he slid his tongue into the recesses of her mouth. The kiss deepened. At some level he was aware that he was hot and sweaty and less than prepared for romance.

But against all odds, this was something more. Visceral. Honest. Intense. They met as equals. Haunted by the past. Yearning for a future. He wrapped his arms around her back, lifting her onto her tiptoes to better reach her mouth.

"Are you okay, Ellie?" he asked, the words hoarse.

Her answer was to press even closer. "Tell me you want me," she said. "Make me believe it."

If that was all he needed to do to please her, the job was easy. "Every damn day since you came back." He nibbled the side of her neck. "I used to dream about this," he muttered. "When we were kids. But you were dating your way through half of the boys in our sophomore class."

He felt her smile. "That's not very complimentary."

"Of course it is. Every guy I knew would have killed for the chance to be your boyfriend."

"Not you."

That silenced him. It was true. He'd been too afraid of losing her altogether to risk anything intimate. At least not until the very end, right before his accident. And then afterward, Ellie had asked for what he couldn't or wouldn't give. Even now, the secret he was keeping from her gnawed away at him.

Ellie gasped, probably because he barely gave

her a chance to breathe in between kisses. His body was taut and hungry, all the blood racing south. His sex was hard and ready. The evidence was impossible to hide in his current clothing.

"Ellie, sweetheart. Enough."

She clung to him, shaking her head vehemently. "Don't stop me. I might have an episode."

"Brat." He chuckled helplessly, even as he felt her fingernails scrape over his nipples. "We can't do this. Not now, anyway. It's too risky. Too soon."

Nine

Ellie knew he was right. But she was so aroused that she shivered with wanting him. He made her feel alive and whole and happy. And it had been so long, so very long since she had felt any of those things.

But she wasn't being fair to Conor. He was a man. With a powerful libido. What she was asking for was something he wasn't willing to give her. Not because he wasn't interested, but because he cared. That knowledge healed a jagged hurt in her soul. A raw, angry wound that had existed for a very long time.

Forcing herself to release Conor, she stepped

back, cupping her hot cheeks with her hands. "I'm sorry."

He shook his head. "I don't want to hear those words anymore. Whatever we have…whatever we are…we'll figure it out."

"You sound so sure."

"Maybe I'm good at bluffing."

His wry grin threatened to melt her into a puddle. Her heart felt more serene than it had in a long time. She was willing to wait, content in the knowledge that the world wasn't going to cave in on her if she didn't hold everything together.

Still, they were both only seconds away from doing something they might regret. Especially given the fact that Emory would soon be wailing for attention. To lighten the mood, she shoved her hands in her back pockets. "What does a girl have to do to get fed around here?"

The relief on Conor's face was almost comical. To give the man his due, he was walking on eggshells around her. Who knew what the doctors had told him and Kirby.

"I will talk about things," she said impulsively. "I swear. I just need time."

Conor's smile didn't quite reach his eyes. "Take all the time you need."

* * *

Considering how the day had begun, Ellie's first evening at Conor's home passed extremely well. Emory enjoyed exploring his new environment. The baby kept the dinner hour from being awkward. Afterward, Conor insisted on helping with the very physical parts of Emory's nighttime routine.

Ellie stood in the doorway of the bathroom watching the big, muscular man juggle the slippery little naked boy. It was comical and sweet and totally unfair. How was a woman supposed to keep her senses when faced with such a scene of domesticity?

Emory's gurgles of laughter when Conor made faces at him were precious and wonderful. She had missed her baby terribly. The hours she spent in Silver Glen's hospital were the first time she had ever been away from him overnight.

She had been sobered and abashed when the doctor explained her situation. She'd also been embarrassed. She was a normal, competent, well-educated woman. It was hard to accept that she had let herself get so close to the edge that her reason had momentarily snapped.

Conor shot her a glance over his shoulder. "Grab me his towel, will you?"

Reaching for the turquoise terry-cloth wrap with the doggy ears, she held it open in her arms while Conor lifted Emory out of the tub and handed him to her. Emory gave her the sweetest smile as she bundled him up and dried his little body. No matter what happened in her life, this helpless baby was her responsibility.

Conor glanced down at himself ruefully. "I'm soaked through to the skin. Let me change and I'll be back."

She nodded, heading for the small room that had become Emory's nursery. Conor had spared no expense in outfitting it. The light maple changing table and rocker matched the bed and dresser. The bedding was blue and green with circus animals gamboling across the fabric.

As she diapered Emory and rubbed his chubby arms and legs with lotion, she pondered the reasons a man might go to such expense for a woman who held no special place in his life. She and Conor were childhood friends. Nothing more. Even upon her return, their relationship had existed primarily because of Kirby and his situation.

The money wasn't really an issue. Conor had plenty of it. But to put all of this together so quickly, he had committed time, as well. And thoughtfulness. Was it because he felt guilty that they had argued?

Emory was old enough now to hold a cup with help. So she sat with him in the rocker and sang songs as he drank his milk. Soon his eyelids were drooping. She laid him in his crib, picked up the monitor, and tiptoed out of the room.

Fabulous smells wafted through the air as she stepped out into the hall. Following her nose, she made her way to the kitchen where she found Conor unpacking restaurant cartons.

His hair was rumpled and he wore an old gray Silver Slopes T-shirt untucked over wrinkled khakis. The Kavanaghs were wealthy. She knew that. She'd seen Conor in a tux and Conor half-naked. But whoever said that clothes made the man was dead wrong.

Conor was Conor. He was comfortable in his own skin. He was strong, both mentally and physically, and though he was powerful and extremely masculine, he had the gift of tenderness.

She knew how easy it would be to fall in love

with him. Too easy. But she had Emory to consider. And there were things Conor didn't know. Things she hadn't told anyone.

Maybe it was cowardly, but for now all she wanted to do was live in the moment. The doctors had prescribed rest. So she would rest. And wallow in Conor's careful attention.

It would be wrong to seduce him. He was determined to do the honorable thing. And maybe he was right. Because if he learned her guilty secrets, he might turn away in disgust.

Chastened by that realization, she was careful to keep her distance as they carried dinner into the dining room.

"Good grief," she said. "You have enough food here for six people. Are we expecting a party?"

Conor shook his head. "No. But I'm a fan of good leftovers, and I don't know what you like anymore." He sat down beside her.

As she dug into her teriyaki chicken, she tried not to notice the fact that his hip almost touched hers. Occasionally his arm brushed hers as he reached for a second helping or tried something new. It took an effort not to flinch or move away.

I don't know what you like anymore. It was

true. The attraction that simmered between them was likely nothing more than the remnants of a teenage relationship that was long gone. She and Conor didn't really even know each other at all. She had secrets. No doubt he did, as well.

Secrets made a bad foundation.

On the other hand, if all she wanted…all *he* wanted…was to scratch an itch, did it really matter if they bared their souls? People indulged in purely physical encounters all the time. Maybe she and Conor could have sex and that would be it.

When he leaned forward to snag a dinner roll, she inhaled his scent. Not something as easily identifiable as aftershave, but a subtle fragrance, a mix of laundry detergent and warm skin.

As unobtrusively as possible, she put a few more inches between them. Suddenly, the idea of spending a few weeks in this house, much less a few days, seemed daunting. She finished up her meal and stood to carry her plate to the kitchen. "I think I'll go to bed and read," she said, feeling panicky for no discernible reason.

Conor stood, as well. "Are you feeling okay?" he asked, concern etched on his face.

"I'm fine. A little tired."

He followed her to the kitchen, a silent presence at her back. Once she had deposited her things in the dishwasher, she gave him a small smile. “I’ll see you in the morning.”

She fled to her room and closed the door behind her, leaning back against it and putting her hands over her face. Maybe she *was* losing her mind. She didn’t know what she wanted. Part of her craved the physical oblivion of Conor’s lovemaking. The other part, the more rational part, reminded her that she was a responsible parent…and that she didn’t deserve to be happy.

After a hot shower, she went through her nightly rituals. At the vanity, she sat and brushed her hair the obligatory one hundred strokes. The ends needed a good trimming. But when was she supposed to find the time? Being a mom meant squeezing every available moment out of the day.

She called Kirby to reassure him that she was fine. He questioned her with a doctor’s thoroughness, but when he told her he was worried about her, it was her brother speaking, her twin. Convincing him she was well and happy was not easy, particularly since she wasn’t at all sure she was telling the whole truth.

When she climbed into bed and plucked a book off the nightstand, it was still not even nine o'clock. The historical novel she was reading was good, but it had been more than a week since she last picked it up and she had lost the threads of the story. Tossing it aside, she hunkered down in the covers and turned out the light.

Exhaustion rolled over her in suffocating waves. Her head ached. Jangled emotions kept her brain spinning. She needed to make sense of her life. And leaning on Conor wasn't the answer.

But she felt so alone…

Conor flipped channels on the TV, wishing he could go for a walk. But he was reluctant to leave the house with guests under his roof. When his cell phone buzzed, he wasn't surprised to recognize Kirby's number.

He answered on the first ring. "Hey, Kirby. What's up?"

"How is she really?"

"I take it you talked to her?"

"For five minutes. She put on a good show. But I've known my sister a very long time. She doesn't like showing weakness."

"She headed off to bed early. I couldn't decide if it was because she felt bad or because she doesn't feel comfortable with me."

"Maybe she thinks her attraction to you is being disloyal to Kevin."

Conor's stomach clenched. He'd had the same thought. "I wouldn't say this to anyone else, but honestly, Kirby, I feel like I'm damned if I do and damned if I don't."

"I trust you."

"Great." Conor snorted. "I don't know whether to be flattered or creeped out. I'm not in the habit of discussing my intimate relationships with *anyone*, much less a family member of the female in question."

"At least you're contemplating sex. I haven't been with a woman since before my accident."

Conor gripped the phone, almost sure that his buddy hadn't meant to blurt that out. After a long moment of silence, he sighed. "That bites."

"Yeah. Tell me about it." Kirby's voice was a combination of resignation and frustration. "What am I supposed to do? Tell her to wait a minute while I pop off my foot? Or leave it on and hope it doesn't feel weird to her? I'm screwed."

"Or not."

Kirby burst out laughing. "Thanks for the help."

"Anytime, man. Anytime. But seriously, Kirby. When the right woman comes along, it won't matter."

"You sound awfully sure of that for a guy who's single and sleeping alone."

"Fine. I'll take my pep talks elsewhere. And for the record, I'm single *by choice*. Has anyone ever told you your bedside manner sucks?"

"If you end up in my hospital, I swear I'll be nice to you. But until then..."

"Promises. Promises."

They talked a little longer and then agreed that Kirby would drop by in the morning. Conor ended the call with a smile on his face. He had plenty of friends. Lots of friends, actually. But there was something about a guy who had known you since you were a snotty-nosed kid. Kirby understood Conor and vice versa.

It was wonderful to have him back in Silver Glen, even if for only a little while.

At ten, Conor walked in his sock feet to Ellie's door and stood there quietly. He couldn't detect any sounds at all. Not that silence was a guarantee she was asleep.

He then moved a few steps down the hall to the other door that accessed the suite…the door to Emory's temporary nursery. All was quiet. He was determined to deal with Emory if the baby awoke during the night.

The most straightforward approach would have been to ask Ellie for the baby monitor. But she was stubborn, and despite doctor's suggestions, she was intent on caring for the baby all on her own. The chances of her surrendering the monitor so she could get a good night's sleep were slim to none.

With a sigh, he returned to the living room, knowing that he would never be able to sleep at this hour. He sat on the sofa, elbows on his knees, and dropped his head in his hands. What was he going to do about Ellie?

Maeve Kavanagh had started from an early age teaching her boys how to respect women. Perhaps because their father, Reggie, had been feckless and selfish, Maeve had instilled in her sons the two *Rs*—responsibility and respect. That last one covered a multitude of sins. Respect for the environment. Respect for the less fortunate. Respect for your fellow man in general. But, most of all, respect for feminine vulnerability when it came to physical relationships.

Conor would never under any circumstances coerce a woman who said no. But what about a woman who said yes? A woman who had borne more than her share of tragedy and heartache recently. Who was strong in every way, but momentarily needed protection and support.

What was a man supposed to do in that situation?

A faint noise alerted him to the fact that he was no longer alone. Standing in the arched doorway was Ellie. Hair mussed. Feet bare. Eyes shadowed with dark smudges. Her expression was a cross between distress and defiance.

"Ellie." Great. His speech had been reduced to single-word sentences.

She tugged her thin turquoise robe tightly across her chest, perhaps unaware that she was giving him an even nicer view of her breasts. Particularly the way the nipples thrust against the soft fabric.

"I can't sleep," she said.

Was that a statement? Complaint? Request for help?

He stood and rubbed his chin, realizing that he had forgotten to shave that morning. In the hustle and hurry of making sure the house was ready before he dashed off to the hospital, he'd been focused on his concern for Ellie.

"Would you like some warm milk?" Great. Now he sounded like an old geezer.

Her golden-red hair seemed to glow, making her lack of color more pronounced. She shook her head. "No. Thank you."

"A shot of whiskey?"

Again she declined. "I can't. Because of the medication I'm taking."

"Ah." He'd exhausted his repertoire of sleep aids. Except for heart-pounding, wildly orgasmic, hot-monkey sex. And that was not on the list of approved rehabilitative activities for a woman who had suffered a blow to the head.

"Would you like to sit down?" He couldn't read her.

Ellie shook her head, still glued in the doorway, her lower lip trembling.

A flash of genuine anxiety drew him across the

room. "Talk to me, Ellie. Tell me what's wrong. What do you want me to do for you?" He unfolded her arms and took both her hands in his. Her fingers were cold.

Without overthinking it, he drew her into his embrace, ruefully aware that his body instantly responded to hers.

She buried her face in his chest. "It's stupid," she muttered.

Her hair smelled like flowers. "Tell me, anyway." Why did she have to feel like perfection when he held her? The physical connection couldn't make up for all the unspoken realities that lurked between them with the deceptive nature of quicksand.

"I had nightmares," she whispered. "In the hospital. Kirby and Kevin were falling off the mountain. Again and again. I'm afraid to go to sleep." She paused. "Come to bed with me, Conor. Please. Not for sex, I swear."

Ten

Conor wondered what he had done in a prior life to deserve this kind of torture. But denying her was not an option.

"Of course," he said quickly. He suspected that her toes were as cold as her fingers. So he scooped her up in his arms and carried her to the bedroom. The large bed was mostly untouched. On Ellie's side, though, it was easy to see that she had been restless.

Tossing back the sheet and spread, he laid her down gently and covered her up. After kicking off his shoes, he climbed onto the mattress, scooted past her, and leaned against the headboard with a sigh. The room was dimly lit. He yawned, feeling peace envelop him, despite his acute awareness of the woman at his side.

As always, the paradox perplexed him. How could he want her so badly and yet be soothed simply to lie by her side?

Out of the corner of his eye he saw Ellie wriggling to remove her robe. He held one sleeve until she managed the exercise. Now she was clad in nothing more than a sheer gown that was half-a-dozen shades lighter in color and a hundred times more provocative.

Though he could only see her from the waist up, that was enough.

He closed his eyes. "I would sing to you if I could," he joked. "But we'd both regret that."

"I don't know that regret is such a bad thing. At least it means we've lived." She took his attempt at humor and tossed it back in his court.

"I've lost a lot of things I've cared about, Ellie. And believe me, I've lived and breathed regret."

"Your career?"

He stared straight ahead, his brows drawn tight. "Yeah."

"I'm sorry about that," she said quietly. "I feel like Kirby and I let you down. You'd barely been home from the hospital two weeks when we moved away. But most of all, I'm sorry for breaking up with you after your accident. I was so damned scared, and I thought if I gave you a choice of skiing or me, you would pick me."

"We weren't even really a couple," he said, his throat tight. "No apologies necessary." Those had been dark days. Though he'd never admitted it to anyone, when he'd been trussed up in that hospital—his body broken and in jaw-clenching pain—there had been a second or two when he hadn't wanted to live. Even now it was hard to talk about it. "Tell me what you think Kirby will do in terms of picking a place to practice."

It was a clumsy change, of course, but he hated the feeling that she was poking around in his psyche.

Ellie inched closer to him, though they were still divided, her below the covers and him above. "I think he's leaning toward Miami. We've talked recently about buying a house together. I don't want to go back to work until Emory is in school, but when I'm ready, Miami has a big enough international population to make my skill set valuable."

"And in the meantime?"

"Kirby will be working long hours. It will be nice for him to come home to a hot meal and an organized household."

"I doubt he expects you to wait on him hand and foot."

"Of course not. But the arrangement will be good for both of us. Emory is going to need a strong male influence in his life."

"And if Kirby falls in love?"

He felt Ellie go still. "Then I'll find my own place, of course."

Her voice was small and hurt. He was goading her deliberately, because the thought of her moving so far away a second time made him want to punch something. "Go to sleep," he said gruffly. "I won't leave you."

Ellie trembled, though she was plenty warm. What did Conor want from her? He'd made it sound as if a move to Miami was a personal betrayal. Was that how he'd felt when all three of them were only sixteen?

She closed her eyes, desperate for rest, but more desperate to crack the code that accessed Conor Kavanagh's protective shield. One moment he treated her with the avuncular platonic attention of a relative. The next he exuded an unmistakable vibe of sexual need.

Pretending to be asleep, she counted the cadence of his breathing. Out of the corner of her eye she could see that he had his hands folded across his abdomen. He had snagged two of the extra pillows and tucked them behind his back.

What was he thinking?

She was curled on her side, facing him. If she moved her hand, she could touch his hard thigh.

"Conor," she whispered.

He never flinched. "Yes?"

"Will you get under the covers and hold me?"

The seconds that ticked away before he answered were crushing.

When Emory made it to his six-month birthday and when Kirby finally finished all his surgeries, she'd naively thought she had reached her lowest point and was on the way back up, but this week had taught her differently.

Conor nodded. "Sure."

He rolled off the bed, folded the covers back and climbed in beside her. Instantly, she felt his body heat, as hot and wonderful as a furnace on an icy winter night. Still, he made no move to get any closer.

Knowing his scruples, she took the initiative. He was on his back. Scooting against him, she rested her bent knee across his leg and put her head on his arm.

When he shifted to wrap that same arm around her, she wanted to cry. Her parents had been with her after Kevin's death. And they'd stayed for a month until Kirby was past the danger point. But then they had returned to the jungle and to their work.

Kirby had been too ill to hold his sister and comfort her. Emory was yet to be born. Friends didn't know what to say to a woman who had lost so much. So she pretended she was strong. She had moved from one day to the next, doggedly doing what had to be done.

She would never forget Kirby sleeping in a chair during her labor and delivery. He'd been on crutches at that point, twenty pounds lighter and still recovering from a recent surgery. Mrs. Porter had missed the baby's birth. She'd contracted malaria in the jungle, and her husband had stayed in Bolivia to care for her.

After Ellie had been in labor for twenty-six hours, Kirby had passed out on the floor beside Ellie's bed and been admitted to a hospital room of his own. A night nurse with a drill sergeant attitude had coached Ellie through the final hours, smiling triumphantly alongside the exhausted mother when little Emory emerged, healthy and whole.

Now, in Conor's arms, all of that seemed like a dream. Ellie's eyes grew heavy. "This is nice," she said, the words slurred.

He kissed her forehead. "Sleep, Ellie. Just sleep."

When she surfaced the next time, the room was filled with the gray light of predawn. And it was raining. Hard. The steady drumming on the roof brought with it a sensation of coziness and safety.

Conor snored softly beside her. For a moment, she barely recognized the sensation that slid through her veins in a drowsy river. Happiness. Contentment. Hope.

Big emotions to hang on one brief moment in time. Conor was being nice to her, that's all. The challenges she faced still existed outside this bed. Even so, she was prepared to live in the now.

With her eyes closed, she inhaled the scent of him. Conor. Friend. Confidant. *And lover?*

Carefully, she slid her right hand beneath his warm cotton shirt where it had rucked up at his waist. His taut, flat abdomen invited a woman's touch. He was so real. So alive.

He moved restlessly in his sleep. Chagrined, she rolled away.

Though she was very still in the aftermath of her impulsive behavior, she had awakened the beast. He snagged her wrist and dragged her close.

His eyes heavy lidded, he gazed at her. "I can't say no to this anymore, Ellie. Because I want you more than my next breath. I'm not the man you need forever… But I could be the guy you need today…if that's all you want."

He would never know the courage it took to answer. "Yes." As he rolled on his side to face her, her fingertips found his collarbone, his sternum, the soft trail of hair that bisected his chest and led to his belt buckle.

Conor's lopsided smile encompassed a wry awareness of all the reasons this was a bad idea. "I've wanted you since I was fifteen."

"With an extensive time-out in between," she pointed out.

Her heart pounded in a jerky rhythm as she deftly unbuttoned the single fastening at his waistband.

"Years. Minutes. Who cares?" He kissed her hard, his hips moving restlessly against hers. His breathing was harsh and his movements jerky as his hands caressed her breasts through a layer of fabric.

"Conor…" She whispered his name, caught up in a wave of desire so intense it left her dizzy and disoriented.

He bit her earlobe, the little spritz of pain sparking through her nervous system. "I'm here."

She pressed her hand, palm flat, against his sex…only a couple of layers of fabric between her skin and his. Guilt and pleasure and anticipation jostled for position in her few remaining brain cells.

Beneath her fingertips, he flexed and hardened. He groaned as she stroked him. The erection that rose hot and hard beneath her touch was not shy. Conor shifted in the bed. "Ellie…"

The way he said her name, all gruff and demanding, made her hot. She slid her fingers beneath the edge of his pants, not far enough to touch the evidence of his excitement, but enough to toy with the sensitive skin around his navel.

She moved half on top of him so she could nibble the side of his neck. "The doctor said exercise would be good for me…as a stress reliever." So far he was letting her set the pace, but she had no illusions. His whole body was tensed for action.

Lowering his zipper slowly, she heard his sharp intake of breath. Her hand closed around him, feeling the urgency in his sex. Warm skin over hot male need. Elemental. Timeless.

He cursed softly, even as he swelled in her grasp. "There's no going back, Ellie. Not after this." It was a warning, but since his hands kneaded her bottom as he said it, she didn't put much stock in the words.

She kissed him full on the mouth, exulting when he took control and pulled her tight against his chest. "I don't want to go back," she panted. "The past is over. I want to be selfish and irresponsible."

"You don't know how."

He kissed like a dream. For a split second, she

hated all the faceless women he'd practiced with. But then his tongue stroked her lower lip and she forgot to care. He held her chin with one big hand, tilting her face toward his, sliding a finger around her jaw to play with her tiny gold hoop earring.

It would be really embarrassing to come from nothing more than a man touching her earlobe.

"Um, Conor?" she panted.

"Yeah?" He released her and levered upward to rip his shirt over his head.

"I'm on the pill. For medical reasons. And I haven't slept around."

He chuckled hoarsely, kissing the spot where her neck and shoulder met. "I think I knew that. The last part, I mean. You don't have to worry about me, Ellie."

When his teeth raked her skin, she thought she might swoon. Did women do that anymore? Or only ones that slept with Conor?

Her gown was strangling her. And she was hot. So hot.

Conor gripped the thin fabric. "Are you attached to this?"

Her nightwear was made of sheer Swiss cotton. Imported. Very expensive. Something she'd bought last year to remind herself she was still a woman and not only a mom. "Not particularly."

Two big hands ripped the batiste from stem to stern. "I've always wanted to do that." She thought he was joking until she saw the intent look on his face. He zeroed in on her breasts, his gaze slightly awed. "You're beautiful, Ellie…so damned beautiful it makes me ache."

She wanted to say *thank you* or *that's sweet*, but all she could do was close her eyes and feel. His touch was reverent but determined. Each of his hands was large enough to cup one of her full breasts.

Torn between wanting to savor his tenderness and needing to hurry him along, she hung teetering on the edge of something amazing…something she had wanted for a very long time.

She bit her lip. Speaking seemed unnecessary under the current conditions, but if she didn't say something, she was worried that Conor might linger too long. "Foreplay is great and all that," she said, "but I wouldn't mind if you moved on to the main course." Her comment was a masterpiece of rational, polite discourse.

Conor raised a single eyebrow. “Impatient much?”

She kicked his ankle. “I’ve waited a long time for this.”

“Not as long as me,” he muttered, finally understanding the urgency of the situation. Lifting his hips, he shed his pants and cotton boxers with the efficiency and speed of a seasoned athlete.

Now they were both naked.

He tossed back the covers and reclined on his side. “I think we should savor this.”

“No.” She lurched at him, managing to bump into a rather impressive body part. “Please tell me you’re joking.”

“I was.” He laughed, wincing when she climbed on top of him to smother his face with kisses. “But then again, anticipation is half the pleasure.”

Ellie placed her hands, palm flat, on his shoulders. “No. It’s not. Pleasure me, Conor. Prove me wrong.”

It was difficult for a man to make smart decisions when his brain was oxygen deprived. He *could* blame it on the fact that Ellie sat on his chest squashing the air out of him. Or on the fact that his erection was as rigid and solid as the proverbial iron spike because all the available O2 had rushed south in his bloodstream.

But the truth was, when he looked at Ellie naked, he forgot how to breathe.

Pleasure me, Conor. He wanted to. God knew he wanted to. Despite his arousal, some nasty little portion of his brain reminded him that this was likely the first time she'd had sex since her husband died.

What if he couldn't make her climax? What if she became so distraught in the midst of physically connecting that she had another breakdown? What if she cried because she missed her husband?

Damn it to hell and back.

He could pretend Ellie was his teenage fantasy. Maybe that would erase the troubling questions. But he wanted the adult Ellie. The accomplished, beautiful, multidimensional woman who spoke several languages and had a baby and smiled at him with the sweet openness that told him some things *never* change.

He gripped her hips. "You mean the world to me, Ellie." He laid it out there, not wanting her to think this was a toss away…an insignificant moment in the midst of a rough time in her life.

Above him, her hair fell like silken rain. "I want you, Conor," she said, her smile both tremulous and confident. "Both the boy I knew and the man you are."

Unwittingly, her words echoed his thoughts. "Did you ever wonder?" he asked. "About us being intimate?"

She grinned. "Of course. I was jealous of you and Kirby. You were both so close, and I wanted that with you."

"But the one time you and I tried to be more than friends, you said I wasn't the kind of guy you wanted."

"I was wrong." Her little wiggle scalded his nerve endings.

He shifted her, lifting her upward only to pull her down as he joined their bodies. When she slid onto his sex, taking him deep, he closed his eyes. Little flashes of light pulsed with the beat of his heart.

She was tight and hot and utterly perfect.

Ellie leaned back on her hands, driving him the slightest bit crazy. She placed her feet flat on the bed and used the purchase to ride him slowly. "I'll bet you know a lot of kinky stuff about sex. Admit it."

He gasped, already on the cusp of coming. "Don't talk," he begged.

Up. And down. "I thought men liked talking. At least during sex."

"I like it." His jaw ached from clenching his teeth. "But I don't need any more stimulation at the moment."

Inward muscles gripped his shaft. "Are you saying we're good together?"

"No."

She pretended to be hurt, when he knew damned well that she could tell he was straining to keep from crossing the finish line. "That's not very gallant." Leaning forward, she nipped one of his flat nipples with sharp teeth. "I'm doing the best I can."

From somewhere he found the presence of mind to touch her where it mattered. His targeted caress turned his smart-mouthed tormentor into a needy beggar. Sprawling on his chest, she cried out. "Do something, Conor. I'm dying."

He rolled them instantly, shoving her onto her

back, driving so deep he saw a red haze. Primal male urges took over. "Whatever you want, Ellie. Whatever you need."

After that, there were no words, no time-out, no playful sex talk.

There was only Ellie.

Eleven

Conor surfaced groggily, feeling as if he had finished a challenging downhill slope. His muscles quivered. His body was lax. His breathing struggled to find a normal rhythm.

And then it came again. The sound that had awakened him. Emory.

It was seven-thirty. The kid was probably starving.

Conor moved surreptitiously, sliding out of bed and pulling on his underwear and pants. Ellie slept like the dead, on her back, both arms flung over her head. She had whisker burn on her throat.

Her naked body was mesmerizing. A painter or sculptor would find her an irresistible subject.

Though Ellie complained about her weight, Conor loved her curves. Full breasts, shapely thighs, a butt that was made for a man's hands.

She was real and warm and feminine in every way.

When Emory's babbles escalated, Conor knew he had to move fast if he wanted Ellie to get more sleep. In the baby's room, he scooped up the warm, sweetly scented toddler and nuzzled his belly. "Hey, little man. Let's get you a clean diaper, and Uncle Conor will find you something to eat."

Emory's eyes were huge as he sucked his fist. Conor managed the diaper change without incident. Once the soft pajamas were re-snapped in the careful sequence that required an engineering degree, the two of them escaped down the hall.

Tucking Emory into the newly purchased high chair, Conor grinned. "You're a cute kid."

Emory's response was a babbling string of syllables accompanied by drool. His sunny smile made a guy wonder if kids weren't worth the hassle after all.

Breakfast was easy. Dry Cheerios. Milk. Chopped up banana. At this rate, Conor would qualify as a baby nutritionist. While Emory polished off the food on his tray, Conor started the coffeepot. Yawning and rubbing a hand over his bare chest, he thought about the woman he'd left behind in the bed. Soft skin. Soft body. Soft everything.

Bad mistake. Now he had a boner. And it was going to be a very long day. Unless Emory took a nap. That had possibilities.

When Ellie appeared in the kitchen doorway a half hour later, she was wearing Conor's T-shirt. It had never looked so good. The neckline gaped, exposing the very spot he had nibbled only hours before.

The fact that she had supplemented the outfit with a pair of khaki shorts was not a great fashion choice in his opinion. He would have been fine with undies only. Or nothing at all beneath. But since Kirby was coming over at an unspecified time, it was probably a good thing that his sister had shown decorum.

Ellie's expression was hard to read. He'd hoped for a smile. Instead, she seemed abashed. Reluctant to meet his eyes. Keeping his face in neutral, he masked his disappointment. Mornings after were not always easy, especially since he and Ellie had made a big change in their relationship last night.

"I cook a mean waffle," he said. "Are you hungry?"

She nodded. "With eggs and bacon?"

He grinned. "Of course."

While Ellie sat with Emory and entertained her son, Conor threw together the meal. He'd built this house for the solitude and the peace. It was disconcerting to realize that having Ellie and Emory here exposed the fact there might be other more important things to consider.

Family. He was one of seven kids. And he loved his brothers. His mom was a sweetheart, and his dad, despite his many faults, had been a fun parent until he disappeared.

Conor had never really contemplated building a nest. He played hard and worked hard, and his recreational choices involved the kind of risk-taking adrenaline that made him feel alive. Ellie's rejection early on had taught him that few women wanted a long-term relationship with a man like him. He was okay with that. Mostly. Responsibilities tied a man down. He wasn't opposed to that lifestyle. Someday.

When he set a plate in front of Ellie, she put her hand on his arm. "Thank you, Conor." She looked up at him with a smile, a smile that knocked him off kilter.

"For the food?"

"Of course." But the mischief dancing in her eyes told a different story. Suddenly, every second of their predawn romp played in his head in vivid color.

"You're welcome," he muttered. "Eat your eggs before they get cold." He fixed his own plate and took the seat across from her, on the other side of Emory's high chair.

Silence reigned in the pleasant, sunny kitchen as they made short work of their meals.

Emory served as an innocent buffer. It was easier to interact with him than to deal with the fallout from what had happened. And damn it, what *had* happened? A change in the status quo for sure, but it was no big deal. He and Ellie had always enjoyed each other's company. They had merely taken their friendship one step farther.

It was late morning when Kirby made an appearance. In the meantime, Ellie had disappeared into her suite, ostensibly to bathe Emory and get him dressed for the day. As far as Conor could tell, she was hiding out.

Kirby looked good when Conor answered the front door. His buddy's shoulders were straight, his eyes clear and some of the lines around his mouth had disappeared.

"Come on in."

Kirby sprawled on the sofa, his legs propped on the coffee table. At first glance, you would never know that he wore a prosthesis. He lifted an eyebrow. "Is Ellie here? Or did you run her off?"

Conor had put on a shirt, but other than that, he was still in climb-out-of-bed mode. He shrugged, dropping onto the love seat across from Kirby. "She's doing something with the baby."

"Did she sleep well?"

Conor kept his gaze steady. "How should I know? She looked okay at breakfast." It was up to Ellie to decide who she told about her physical relationship with Conor. She and her twin shared most everything, but Conor wasn't going to make that call when the subject was such a private one.

"Hey, guys. Emory wants to say hello."

When Ellie walked into the room, Conor had to wonder if she had overheard the conversation.

Kirby patted the seat beside him. "Here, sis. Let me hold my handsome and superintelligent nephew."

Ellie handed him the baby and sat down, curling her legs beneath her. "Your nephew just smeared poo on his changing table."

She grinned as both men winced in unison. They were each so very masculine and assured. But like most bachelors, there were certain aspects of babyhood that stymied them.

As Kirby played a game of peek-a-boo with Emory, Ellie elbowed her brother gently. "How's Grandpa?" she asked. "Is he wondering where I am?"

"I thought he might ask, but he's been pretty fuzzy the last couple of days. The neighbor, Mrs. Perry, offered to check on him a couple of times while I'm up here."

"I should come home," Ellie said, the words impulsive. "You both need me."

Kirby took her hand in his. "I love you, sis. But you're not indispensable. I'm doing better every day. And you need to take it easy. Has Conor been looking after you?"

She felt her face turning red, but Kirby didn't seem to notice. "Of course. He fed Emory and me breakfast, and his housekeeper dropped by earlier to put a pot of chili on the stove. I know it's summer, but Conor and I agreed that it was a *chili* kind of day."

Kirby's face lit up. "Count me in." He glanced at Conor. "Ellie and I grew to appreciate all manner of South American cuisine, but there's nothing like home-cooked comfort food."

Ellie kissed her brother on the cheek and stood. "If you gentleman have the situation under control, I'd love to take a shower."

Kirby looked up at her. "You feeling okay this morning? You look good. You've got some color in your cheeks."

"I'm doing very well. Thank you for asking. Now can we quit referencing my unfortunate meltdown?"

"Did you ever talk to Mom and Dad?"

She nodded. In the hospital she had refused to call them, not wanting to interrupt their work, but once she was about to be released, she had phoned them, playing down the severity of her episode.

It still made her uncomfortable to admit that she had been temporarily addled.

In her luxurious bathroom, she locked the door and stepped into the shower. The water was hot and strong and reviving. She hadn't gotten quite as much sleep as she would have liked.

Standing beneath the pelting spray, it was easy to remember why. There wasn't an inch of her skin Conor hadn't touched. He had made love to her as if they were the last two people on the earth. Out of control. Desperate. As if they might never have another chance.

And she had been equally urgent.

The whole tenor of their coming together really made no sense. Unless both of them, deep down, thought the relationship had an expiration date. She ran a washcloth over her breasts. They were sensitive, the swollen tips almost painful.

For months she had tried to pretend she was a mother first and a woman second. But sooner or later, her body was going to betray her. In fact, it already had…when she'd hit her head on a rock and imagined for a few hours that she was sixteen again.

Is that what she really wanted? To go back in

time and be Conor Kavanagh's girlfriend? Or did she want something real? Something lasting? Something that meant growing and changing and allowing another person into her life?

She was chastened and thoughtful when she rejoined the men. All three males were on the living room floor, Conor and Kirby letting Emory ride them like horses. The baby was ecstatic, chortling and laughing. He grabbed a handful of Conor's hair and pulled.

"Ow!" Conor howled. His pretend indignation made the toddler do it again. Kirby tugged Emory's foot. "Be careful, love. The monster man is gonna get you."

Hovering in the doorway, Ellie watched them play. To see Kirby so happy and engaged was more than she ever could have wished for. Much of the thanks and credit for that transformation went to the man beside him.

Conor had brought such healing to their little circle of three. He'd made Kirby feel whole again. He'd given Ellie the certainty that her future was brighter than her past. He'd proved to Emory that he was an adult to be trusted.

Conor had moved seamlessly into their lives

and worked his magic without fanfare. Was it any wonder that she was falling in love with him? She put a hand to her chest, feeling an odd little twinge. Love wasn't in the cards for her. She thought she had it once, and she lost it. So why try again? Why risk more pain?

Forcing herself to join the playgroup, she dropped onto her knees and tickled Emory's belly. "How's my sweetheart?"

Conor and Kirby exchanged droll looks. "We're fine," Kirby said.

She plucked Emory from Conor's back. "Very funny. There's only one man who has my heart." She kissed her son's head. "How about lunch, munchkin?"

"Yes, please." Conor touched arm lightly. "You stay here. Kirby and I will set everything out."

His fingers lingered, caressing the inside of her elbow. Kirby was already headed toward the kitchen, so the little byplay was private.

"I'm not an invalid," she muttered.

"Let me pamper you, Ellie. It makes me happy." He kissed her quickly, glancing over his shoulder to make sure they were alone.

Though the caress of his lips was brief, the light

touch packed a punch. Or maybe she was already reeling from this morning. "By all means," she said. "Anything to make you happy."

"Anything?" His grin was devilish.

"Go find my brother. Before he eats our share."

To Conor's relief, lunch was fun and happy and blessedly normal. Emory was in a good mood. Kirby's appetite was almost back to normal. Ellie smiled and relaxed. Conor played the clown until he had them all laughing and squabbling like they had as kids and teenagers.

After they finished eating, Kirby grabbed an envelope he'd brought with him handed it to Ellie. "Here are the pictures you wanted me to get printed for Mom and Dad."

"Printed?" In this digital age, Conor was surprised.

Ellie opened the flap of the large brown mailer and flipped through the images. "Mom and Dad don't always have internet service, especially now that they're even deeper in the jungle to open this new clinic. So they like me to send photos they can hang up." She shook her head. "These are only four weeks old, but Emory changes every day."

While Conor took a look, she glanced at Kirby. "If I address this and put a note in, would you have time to mail it on your way back home?"

"Sure. Not a problem."

"Do you have packing tape and scissors, Conor?"

"Yep. My office is just past my bedroom on the same side of the hall. I've got a big rolltop desk. Try the left side, top drawer."

When Ellie disappeared, Kirby sighed. "She looks happy."

"I think you're right. At least I hope so. How long do you think we can keep her here?"

"As long as you and I can convince her it's for the best. My sister is stubborn."

"As are you and I."

Kirby grinned in agreement and opened his mouth to say something, but whatever it was went unsaid. Ellie stormed into the kitchen, her face white…two spots of color high on her cheekbones.

She kicked the leg of Conor's chair, fury in every hair follicle. "You're going to climb Aconcagua?"

Belatedly, he realized that she held a familiar turquoise-and-yellow travel folder. One that he should have hidden far, far away. "Yes." What else could he say? He wasn't going to lie.

"When?"

"Next winter."

She whirled to face her brother. "*You* put him up to this."

Slowly, Kirby stood, a look of consternation on his face. "No."

Conor spoke softly, gauging her reaction with alarm. "I made those arrangements six months ago. Kirby had nothing to do with it."

She wilted suddenly, her anger morphing into perplexed pain as she gazed from one man to the other. "But Kirby must have egged you on, because you haven't cancelled."

Kirby spoke up, shooting Conor a warning look. "This kind of trip costs thousands of dollars. Prepayments that Conor wouldn't get back. Aconcagua is a fabulous adventure. Dozens of people climb it successfully year after year. What happened to Kevin and me was a freak accident. Conor will be fine."

"You don't know that."

Conor remained silent, feeling unaccountably guilty. He'd done nothing wrong, but *damn it to hell*…this wasn't how he wanted Ellie to find out. He'd planned to tell her himself. When the time was right.

Kirby put his arms around Ellie, hugging her close. "Conor is an experienced climber. He's done Kilimanjaro already. He knows what he's doing."

She looked over Kirby's shoulder at Conor, her eyes damp with emotion. "Is this true?"

Conor nodded grimly.

Ellie jerked away from her brother and backed up against the kitchen wall. "It's *both* of you," she said dully. "You don't feel alive unless you're risking your lives. But why don't you think about what it does to the people who love you?"

Kirby scowled. "That's not fair, Ell. I was a single man with all my affairs in order."

"What about me? You had me."

This time it was Kirby who paled. The standoff between siblings lasted for what seemed like hours. Ellie clutched the damning folder to her chest as if it were Pandora's box that couldn't be opened.

Kirby ran both hands through his hair. "I understand what you're feeling. I really do. But driving a car is dangerous. As is climbing into a plane. Life includes risk, Ellie. Just because you lost Kevin doesn't mean that Conor is doomed."

Now she was gray…haunted. "I don't want to talk about Kevin." Her jaw was so tight it must be giving her a headache. Her gaze was stony.

Kirby shook his head, his expression weary. "No. You never do. And that's the problem. That's why you snapped this week, Ell. If you don't deal with what happened, you'll never get past this."

For a moment, Conor thought she might bolt. She reminded him of a doe caught in the woods, not sure which way to run to avoid disaster.

He went to her instinctively, putting himself physically between the twins. The situation had escalated rapidly, and he was afraid one of them might say something that he or she would regret. He'd never forgive himself if his trip caused a permanent rift between his two best friends.

"That's enough, Kirby," he said. "Ellie has had a rough week." Gently, he pried the folder from Ellie's death grip and tossed it on top of the fridge. Taking her hands in his, he chafed them carefully. "Why don't you go put Emory down for his nap?

He's falling asleep in his high chair. And you need to rest, too."

She shook her head, evading his grasp. "I'm leaving." Her voice was a low monotone. "As soon as I pack our things."

Kirby bristled, flushing with anger. "You sure as hell are not. My professional reputation is on the line here. The only reason you were released from the hospital is because I'm a doctor and because Conor promised to keep an eye on you."

"You can't keep me prisoner."

He brother was adamant. "I can for the next six days. After your checkup next week, as long as they clear you, you'll be free to do whatever you want. But until then, you're staying here in this house. End of story."

Conor suspected that if Ellie had been a hundred percent she would have gone head-to-head with her brother in a defiant showdown. But, given her current emotions, she couldn't manage it.

"I hate both of you," she said, her voice breaking.

Twelve

"That went well."

Kirby's moody scowl reflected Conor's feelings exactly. "She must have loved him very much."

"Yeah. I guess she did. But she can't grieve forever. It isn't healthy."

"Everyone faces loss differently. When my father disappeared, the end wasn't clean. First there were the months of not knowing. Then finally, a court order declaring him dead. My mother held it together because she had seven children. I'm sure I was too young to fully appreciate what she went through. But all I remember is the way she smiled and hugged us and swore that everything would be okay."

"I failed Ellie," Kirby said. "I should have been able to help her through Kevin's death."

"You were fighting a battle of your own. It's my turn to help her."

Kirby left soon afterward. Conor found himself alone and angry. A cloud settled over the house…as if someone had died. And in fact, that was pretty much the situation at hand. Even if it *had* been a long time ago. In the grand scheme of things, eighteen months could seem like the blink of an eye.

For Ellie, the pain of losing Kevin must be as raw and fresh as if it had happened yesterday. Finding Conor's travel plans would have brought it all back. She was suffering. And he wanted to comfort her. But, ironically, he was the person least qualified to do that.

The day was a thousand hours long. He felt honor-bound to stay close. Perhaps to help with the baby. Perhaps to look after Ellie if today's confrontation caused her to relapse.

He was no shrink, but he wondered if the fact that Kirby was finally on the road to recovery, both physically and mentally, had somehow given

Ellie's subconscious permission to drop her heavy load. For months and months she'd had to be strong for her brother while at the same time undergoing unbelievable stress of her own.

Now that Kirby was better, Ellie had frayed a bit at the seams. And, unwittingly, Conor had weakened the very fabric of her existence.

What was his next move? He wasn't a fan of the sit-and-wait approach. He liked to plan a course of action and go with it.

But Ellie made that hard. She literally hid out in her suite with the baby. Though Conor felt foolish for doing so, he listened at the door every half hour to make sure he could hear her voice. That was a great plan in theory. But with the baby napping—Conor peeked in the nursery to make sure—there was no need for Ellie to converse.

When his overactive imagination got the better of him, Conor cracked *her* bedroom door, as well, and spied to see if she was okay. The sight that met his gaze wrenched his heart. Ellie was curled up in a ball on top of the covers, her hand pressed against her mouth.

He thought she was asleep, but he couldn't be sure. Quietly, he eased the door shut and walked away.

* * *

Ellie knew the exact moment that Conor looked in on her. And she knew when he closed the door and retreated. Though it was stupid, she couldn't bring herself to get into the bed properly. She and Conor had made love on those sheets. The experience had been wonderful. Poignant. Utterly satisfying.

And then he had betrayed her.

If you surveyed a hundred people and told them the tale, ninety-nine of them would probably say she had overreacted. But the hundredth one would understand. She had trusted Conor with her body and with her heart, though he didn't know that. To hear that he planned to climb the very mountain that had taken so much from her and from Kirby was unfathomable.

She wanted to rail at him and beat her fists on his chest. But Conor owed her no explanations. He was a free agent. One who knew that Ellie and Kirby were only passing through Silver Glen.

Why should Ellie's opinions or feelings bring any weight to bear on his actions?

Nevertheless, she felt the rip in her heart and filed it away with all the other pain. Pretty soon she was going to suck it up and admit that life in general was like playing the roulette wheel. The house always won.

She could beg Conor not to go, but she had tried that approach half a lifetime ago and failed. Even if she told him how she felt, there was still the matter of her guilty secret. The truth ate away at her, eroding her confidence.

Giving a man the silent treatment was a lot more effective when you weren't living in his house. By five o'clock, the walls of the suite, lovely though they were, began to close in on her. Emory was fractious and not to be consoled. They were both hungry.

With a mental white flag of surrender, Ellie put on a clean outfit, changed the baby and his clothes, and went in search of her host. She found him sitting on the front porch, his boot-shod feet propped on the railing, hands tucked behind his head.

She propped the baby on her hip. "I'm sorry I got so upset. Your life is your life. I don't have any right to criticize or pass judgment."

His feet dropped to the floor and he sat up straight. "And last night?"

"What about last night?" She kept her expression impassive, but it was an effort.

"When a man and a woman do what we did, it gives each of them implied rights."

She shrugged. "I don't think so. We were curious. We wanted to see if there was more than a spark."

"And was there?"

His eyes were dark and turbulent. Despite his seemingly relaxed pose when she stepped outside, his big frame vibrated with a combative edge.

She chose her words carefully. "Of course there was. We've shared a friendship that made us almost family."

"You're Kirby's sister, not mine. I *wanted* you, Ellie. I still do. Even knowing there's a good chance you're in love with another man. But if all you're doing is killing time until you jet off to some exotic city to start a new life with your brother and your kid, then I'd just as soon pass."

"That's not what you said this morning."

"As I recall, we didn't do a lot of talking."

"What do you want from me?" she cried, her chest tight and her eyes gritty.

Conor shook his head wearily. "Something you

aren't willing or able to give, Ellie. Let's chalk last night up to an impulsive mistake. You've got your own demons to battle. I have a few of my own. We'd just make each other miserable. And life's too short for that."

"Where are you going?" she asked as he strode down the steps and around the side of the house.

The rustle of leaves in the summer breeze was her only answer.

Conor didn't know what to do about Ellie. All his life he'd been a smooth operator when it came to women. Flirt with them. Spoil them. Take a few to bed. But until now he hadn't realized how little those relationships had meant. He'd always been monogamous while involved with someone seriously. When the time came to end it, though, he'd never had his heart broken.

More importantly, he'd done his best to make sure *he* hadn't broken any hearts. He was always up-front with women. If they indicated an interest in home and hearth, he let them down gently and moved on.

Ellie created a whole new category. He was falling for her. And it wasn't some nostalgia-driven emotion from the past, although it was becoming more and more clear that his adolescent feelings for his best friend's sister had been more serious than he knew.

As a teenager he'd been confused by his response to Ellie. He enjoyed her company and considered her as much a friend as Kirby. But he hadn't recognized the sexual undercurrent as an indication of something deeper.

Now, with Ellie back in his life, albeit temporarily, everything clicked. Maybe because he was older and knew what he wanted and needed. Maybe because it was no longer taboo to woo her into his bed.

Sweat trickled down his back as he swung his ax to split a log. The pile of firewood at his side grew rapidly, ready for a season that was still weeks in the future. He liked the physical labor. It helped clear his head. It burned off some of the restless energy that plagued him.

What it didn't do was reveal answers.

Tonight, when Emory was in bed, it was time for Conor to talk straight with his tempestuous houseguest.

* * *

Ellie was both intrigued and on edge when Conor asked her to dress for dinner. She chose a sleeveless champagne silk tank dress that was entirely plain in the front but cut almost to her waist in back. The style made it impossible to wear a bra. Thankfully, her full breasts were firm and high.

She owned a small collection of good jewelry she had inherited from her grandmother Porter. From a glittery pile of bracelets and pendants, she chose a single long strand of pearls. They had been her grandmother's wedding gift from her husband. In today's market, the necklace would be obscenely expensive. To Ellie, the perfectly matched pearls were priceless.

Emory went to bed at seven most nights, so the adults were able to eat in peace. Over the elegant meal served in Conor's seldom-used dining room, they managed civil conversation. It helped that his housekeeper was present. The older woman had prepared a sophisticated version of baked pheasant with fresh summer vegetables as accompaniments.

The table was a work of art. Cream linen cloth,

handmade dishes in shades of saffron and dark brown. Matching chunky candlesticks with beeswax tapers. The silverware was heavy and looked old. In deference to Ellie's concussion, water, not wine, flowed freely throughout the evening, served in amber goblets that surely weighed at least a pound each.

When she complimented the presentation, Conor grimaced. "Not long after I finished the house, my four sisters-in-law took it upon themselves to add what they said were necessary touches. It seemed to make them happy, so I gave them free rein."

"I think they did a great job. The house suits you…and the extra touches, too."

Making small talk with Conor was not easy. Their earlier argument had left them both on edge. Maybe they should always have one of Conor's employees nearby to act as referee or to keep the erotic subtext at bay.

Ellie had deliberately chosen to tamp down her pain and her frustration. Some wild part of her decided to live recklessly. If life was going to continually slap her in the face, she might as well enjoy the bright spots. And Conor Kavanagh was definitely a bright spot.

His dark suit was a masterpiece of understatement. He wore it as comfortably as he did everything else. Perhaps it was his animal grace that made him seem so at home in his own skin. He moved with confidence and concealed power, a beautifully masculine creature, incapable of being tamed.

To her credit, she understood his pursuit of adventure, even if she didn't like it.

After the main course was cleared, they feasted on strawberry shortcake. Ellie groaned, pushing hers aside, half-eaten. "You can finish mine," she said. "I'm stuffed, and besides, I happen to know you have an enviable metabolism."

"I'm shocked, Ellie. Was that an oblique compliment? I should ply you with wine more often."

"It was water, remember?" She knew he was teasing her, but in truth, the room spun ever so slightly. Was she trying to bolster her courage for what might seem an outrageous request?

At last, the quiet, efficient employee said her goodbyes and drove away. The house fell silent. Somewhere outside, a coyote howled in the distance. The sound sent a shiver down Ellie's spine. She was alone with Conor, absolutely alone. His property was so secluded they would have no interruptions.

He tapped a fork on the tablecloth absentmindedly, gazing down at a cup of coffee he hadn't bothered to drink.

Her skin felt hot and tight. She recognized her need for his touch even as she loathed her weakness. She was angry with him. Furious, in fact. For taking his precious life so lightly.

But apparently her libido was not so judgmental.

She wanted to clear the table or wash dishes or put away food…anything to occupy her hands and shatter the bubble of intimacy created by candlelight. But Conor's housekeeper had taken care of every detail. There was nothing for Ellie to do. Nothing but ache for Conor.

"I should go to bed," she said. "Emory will be up early."

Conor lifted his head, his heavy-lidded eyes world-weary and determined. "No games, Ellie. You and I have some things to discuss."

She lifted a shoulder, making the pearls slide across her chest. "I think we've said it all." It didn't escape her notice that Conor's gaze lingered a moment too long on the movement of the necklace and the way it curved around one breast.

Paradoxically, his urbane clothing and suave manners reminded her that beneath the trappings of civilization lay the man who had made love to her with single-minded abandon. She could see the evidence in his tight jaw and arrogant posture.

He was not happy with her.

Well, that was too damn bad. She wasn't happy with him, either.

He leaned back in his chair, lifting his water glass and taking a slow sip, eyeing her over the rim. When he put his drink back on the table, she wanted to crawl across the four feet that separated them and lick the moisture from his beautiful sculpted lips.

Bad girl. Bad Ellie.

Perhaps he could read her mind. Because a glint of amusement broke through his solemn regard. "Here's the thing, Ellie. You and I aren't exactly a match made in heaven. I think we could go further with this if either of us was willing to bend. But since that doesn't seem to be the case, I propose détente."

"Under what conditions?" Her legs quivered.

Beneath the concealing edge of the tablecloth, she pressed a hand to her abdomen, striving unsuccessfully to control the swarm of butterflies that had taken residence there.

"Sex," he said bluntly. "Any way you want it."

"And nothing else?"

"I'm not willing to get serious with a woman who still lives with a ghost in her bed and who won't have me as I am."

The blunt criticism brought quick tears to her eyes. "You don't know what you're talking about," she snapped. "But it's just as well, because I'm not willing to get serious with a man who's a reckless lunatic."

"Thank God we're both on the same page." His sarcasm was biting.

"You don't have to make such a noble sacrifice," she snapped. "I won't be here much longer. Surely you can sublimate your need for sex."

He shrugged. "It's not a need for sex, Ellie. It's a need for you."

Ellie shouldn't have been surprised, but Conor saw shock flicker in her eyes. Tonight she looked like a princess. Her dress managed to conceal just enough to make a man go insane. He wanted to slide his hands over that silk and mold it to her curves and valleys.

Then he wanted to strip her bare.

The pearls were a nice touch. Perhaps he would let her wear those and nothing else.

His collar choked him. His heart racketed away in his chest, belying the fact that his aerobic capabilities were above average. Rising to his feet, he put one hand on the table to steady himself. "Come here," he demanded.

When she stood, he inhaled sharply. "Closer," he said.

She came to within inches of where he was standing, so near he could smell the faint perfume on her skin. "I'm here," she said quietly. "Now what?"

How far would she let him go? "Unbutton my shirt."

One blink of those long, thick eyelashes was her only reaction. Her fingers went to the buttons at his chest and slid them, one at a time, through the buttonholes. When she touched his bare skin in passing, his erection grew harder and his knees grew weak.

When she was done, her hands fell to her sides. She lifted an eyebrow as if to mock him. “Next?”

“Remove my tie.”

Her hair brushed his chin when she reached up to struggle with the knot. At last, she managed to undo it, and then slid the expensive strip of red paisley from around his neck. She held it for a moment, her expression indecisive. Then she reached out and stuffed it in his hip pocket.

Neither of them acknowledged the fact that her fingers made indirect contact with his sex. But Ellie’s cheeks flushed.

He swallowed. “Take off your shoes and bend over the table.” He didn’t really think she would do it. Any second now she would balk.

But he was wrong.

After only a moment’s hesitation, she kicked off her sexy heels and turned her back to him. Carefully sliding the candles and the few remaining cups and glasses to the far end of the table, she then did as he had commanded. Her legs were splayed eight inches or so to keep her balance. She spread her arms above her head, palms down.

Sweet God in heaven.

The couture garment gaped now, the fabric almost sliding off her shoulders. He put one hand at the top of her spine and caressed her from nape to ass. "I like the view," he muttered.

They were both fully clothed, except for her shoes. But he was more aroused than he had ever been in his life. He cleared his throat. "I know you aren't wearing a bra. Is there any other underwear I should know about?"

She gave him a sizzling glance over her shoulder. "Feel free to find out."

The little tease wasn't going to get the upper hand. He planned to drive her wild. Just as soon as he remembered how to breathe.

Carefully, he lifted the silky hem of her dress and crumpled it in his left hand. With his right, he stroked the backs of her thighs. Ellie made a garbled noise and crossed her arms, burying her face.

"Problem?" he asked. This position stoked his desire, sending it spiraling higher.

Ellie shook her head but didn't speak.

He took that as license to continue. With his thumb, he traced the creases at the backs of her knees. Her skin was softer than the fabric in his hand. Releasing the dress, he put both hands on her legs. Her thighs were firm and womanly.

"Don't move," he groaned. "I'm about to discover what's under this dress."

Thirteen

Ellie whimpered and bit down hard on her bottom lip to keep from repeating such an embarrassing sound. She knew Conor had a playful side. But this kinky stuff was a facet of him she hadn't anticipated. He deserved to know the truth about her feelings for Kevin, but she couldn't bring herself to talk about it. Kevin was Emory's father. Conor was Ellie's lover. How had she let her life get so complicated?

When she felt the brush of Conor's fingers between her thighs, she gave up soul-searching. She had spent too many hours thinking and worrying and not enough time enjoying life.

With Conor, that was not going to be a problem.

Scalding heat spread from everywhere he touched. His fingertips were gentle as he explored the center panel of her undies. The satin underpants were bikini cut but not particularly daring. Nevertheless, she suddenly felt like the sexiest woman on the planet.

He pressed gently as he leaned over her and kissed the center of her spine. "This is so much better than fighting," he muttered.

The weight of him on her back stole her breath but in a good way. "Don't bring up touchy subjects," she said, only half joking. "I'm trying to pretend you're my knight in shining armor."

Now, a single finger trespassed beneath the edge of her underwear and stroked gently. She was damp. And needy.

Conor's voice came hoarse and rough, his breath hot on the bare skin of her back. "I've never seen a woman less in need of rescuing. You're strong enough and brave enough to storm any castle. But I'd like to help if you'll let me."

He'd caught her at her weakest moment and said something so damned sweet she wanted to cry. To talk about Kevin's death would make her so vulnerable and naked she was afraid she might shatter and never find all the pieces.

"You *have* helped," she whispered. "You *are* helping."

Conversation ended as he thrust inside her body with first a single finger and then two. She moaned and moved against his hand, caught up in the magic that was Conor.

Suddenly, the weight at her back disappeared. She felt him drag the panties down her legs. He helped her step out of the small piece of cloth.

This morning he had ripped her nightgown. Now he was unbearably tender and gentle with her. Taking her by the shoulders, he brought her upright and turned her to face him. "You can trust me, Ellie."

His face was so serious, so dear. In his eyes she saw echoes of the boy who had been her best friend, along with Kirby. She *did* trust Conor. In almost every way that mattered. But she couldn't trust him not to die.

Lifting onto her tiptoes, she kissed him. His lips were firm and tasted of strawberries. "Take me to bed, Conor."

She wondered if he would have preferred his

own room, but he didn't ask. They could have moved the baby monitor down the hall, but she had to admit that being close to her son made her feel more secure.

They walked hand in hand the short distance to the guest suite. Once inside her bedroom, Conor closed the door and kicked off his shoes. When she would have removed her dress, he stopped her. "Let me."

A short zipper at the base of her spine was designed to allow the dress to slide down over her hips. Conor lowered the tab but went no farther. He faced her, arms loosely around her waist. He kissed her nose, her eyebrows, the spot beneath her ear that made her shiver.

Ellie looked up at him, searching his face for answers. Why did being with Conor seem so very natural and right? She sighed, resting her cheek on his chest. "I wonder what would have happened all those years ago if I had kissed you more than that one time when we were both sixteen."

His hand tangled in her hair. She felt the rumble of his laughter. "Probably something we both would have regretted. I thought about you night and day. If we had done any serious fooling around, I might have imploded. Teenage boys aren't known for their self-control."

"I like the man you've become."

"Careful, sweetheart. All this praise will go to my head."

"I'm serious." She slid her hands inside his shirt. His skin was hot and smooth over hard muscle. There was a part of her that wanted to let Conor erase all of her worries. To lean on him and let him fight her battles. To play the helpless female.

But that was a role she'd never embraced in her life. She and Kirby had been treated as equals by their parents. No special favors for being a girl. She had learned at an early age that tears were unacceptable as a means of getting her way.

In college she had been stunned to watch so many young women manipulate guys with sex. Even as an eighteen-year-old, she had known that was wrong. A man and a woman should stand on equal footing in a relationship. Sex shouldn't be a bargaining chip.

"I'm still dressed," she said, leaning into him and stroking his back. When she slid her fingers into the waistband of his pants, she felt him shudder.

"Is that a complaint?"

"More of an observation."

"I can remedy that."

Carefully, he slid the dress from her shoulders and down her legs, holding her hand so she could step out of it. While she stood naked, he draped the silk over a nearby chair.

He took a step backward and leaned against the dresser, his hot gaze roving from her candy-apple-red toenails to the pulse that beat in her throat. The heat in his regard scalded her. She put her hands over her belly. "Don't stare. I've still got baby weight. I won't ever again be that teenage girl you wanted."

Now he scowled. "Stop it. You have no idea what you're saying. Hell, Ellie." He took her by the wrist and dragged her in front of the mirror. "Look at what I see."

She did look. And her eyes widened at the image of the man in crisp black-and-white. He was sophisticated. Handsome. Compelling. His smile held a dollop of arrogance mixed with the trademark humor that was Conor. "I feel a little at a disadvantage," she croaked.

It was disconcerting to see her nipples furled tightly, as if eagerly awaiting a lover's touch.

Conor moved behind her and encircled her with his arms. When his hands settled on her soft belly, she flinched and tried to shrug free. But he held her easily. “You have a woman’s body, Ellie. A body that created and nurtured life. Do you know how magical that is? Don’t ever apologize for the evidence of your sacrifice. To me, it’s extraordinary.”

She felt the sting of tears and blinked them away, ruefully aware that her emotions were still far too near the surface. “Thank you.” She could barely speak the words.

“Enough serious talk,” he said lightly. But in his eyes she saw a reflection of her own struggle to understand what was happening between them. He scooped her into his arms and carried her to the bed. “Don’t move. I’m coming in after you.”

Laughing softly, she acknowledged something that seemed so simple and yet was so very profound. Conor was fun. With him she felt pieces of her old self coming back. The young woman who had taken Buenos Aires by storm. Studied a handful of languages. Learned about political issues. Snagged fascinating internships. Graduated at the top of her class.

She'd had six job offers on her twenty-second birthday.

All of that seemed like a dream now. She wouldn't trade Emory for all the employment opportunities in the world. But she did want to reclaim her confidence. That—along with her ability to hope—had been decimated in the accident on Aconcagua.

She hadn't been on the mountain that day to witness the freak storm and to see the frantic efforts at search and rescue. But she had a good imagination. Those were the scenes that replayed again and again in her nightmares.

Dragging her thoughts from the grim reality that couldn't be changed, she gave herself up to the pleasure of watching Conor undress. Men did it so differently than women. First the jacket tossed carelessly aside. Then the shirt jerked free of the trousers and the sleeves ripped down the arms.

Conor was clearly impatient, but she wouldn't have minded if the striptease lasted a little longer. Her fascination must have penetrated his focus, because he stopped suddenly. "What?"

She lifted her arms over her head and linked

her hands behind her neck. "Nothing. Just enjoying the show."

His hands went to his fly, unfastening it with a cocky flourish. "I've never been an exhibitionist, but if it turns you on, I'm sure I could drag this out for another half hour."

Sitting straight up in bed, she held out her hand and crooked her finger. "Don't you dare!"

Laughing, he finished the job without ceremony, never even noticing when Ellie's cheeks turned red and her breathing quickened. Once he had dispensed with pants, shoes, socks and underwear, he joined her under the covers, grabbing her up in a bear hug and rolling onto his back with her in his arms, one of his big thighs lodged between hers.

He pulled her head down for a kiss. "I'm sorry I upset you this morning, Ellie."

She noticed he wouldn't say he was sorry that he was going to climb the mountain that had killed her husband and maimed her brother. It was a lie, and Conor never lied. "I'm fine," she said. She didn't want to ruin the mood, and if she told him how much she hated the idea of him putting himself in danger, that's what would happen. "Have I mentioned what a fine specimen of manhood you are? I'm surprised I didn't have to fight off hordes of eager women to make it to your bed."

"The tales of my exploits are greatly exaggerated." His big hands palmed her bottom, squeezing gently. "I'm pure as the driven snow."

"Uh-huh."

He grinned at her, and her heart stopped. *Oh, God. She was so in love with him.* How much more self-destructive could she be?

Conor sobered as if he could read her mind. "Relax, Ellie." He tangled his fingers in her hair. During dinner she'd had it caught up in an antique hair clasp, but somewhere along the way, the delicate ornament had disappeared…right along with her sense of self-preservation.

"I'm relaxed," she said. "Really, I am."

He didn't seem convinced, but when she wiggled against him, his eyes glazed over. He grabbed her knee. "Easy there, darlin'."

"Sorry. Apparently, I'm eager. Or easy. I can't decide which."

"I'll take either. Or both." He palmed her nape. "Close your eyes, Ellie. Let me enjoy you."

His syntax must be wrong, because when he eased her gently onto her back and touched her intimately, *she* was definitely the one enjoying the caress. Conor had gifted fingers. He stroked and petted and plucked until her back arched off the mattress and she slid into an orgasm as sweet and pure as honey.

When she caught her breath and opened her eyes, Conor had fallen onto his back, his gaze trained on the ceiling. It was a very nice ceiling, but surely he had seen it before.

She swallowed, her throat dry. "Um, that was…"

"Maybe not my best work. I should probably try again."

Conor reeled from an extraordinary revelation. He was in love with Ellie. Not *falling* or *on the way* or any other euphemism. He was ass over heels, drowning and reaching for a life raft, crazily, wonderfully in love.

He slung an arm over his face, stunned and trying not to let on.

Ellie was still catching her breath. "You're good at that," she said, the words slurred.

"You inspire me."

"Very funny."

He'd never been more serious in his life. And

never in his life had he been so afraid. He could stand at the top of a wicked European black diamond slope and feel no fear at all. The prospect of plunging into the course was nothing but exhilaration.

For years he had relished proving to himself that he was no longer the kid who had to stay inside and watch as his brothers had all the fun. Each time he accomplished some physical goal, he managed to erase more and more of his constrained childhood. Even now with a bum knee and orders not to ski like a crazy man, he was still tempted to try, just for the fun of it.

But this thing with Ellie…that was another story. He wanted all of her. Not just her body, but her sharp mind, her clever wit, her unwavering loyalty and her love. Lord help him, he wanted her love. But that was the one thing he couldn't have, because that gift had been buried with her dead husband.

He had to pull himself together, or any minute now Ellie was going to see that there was something going on here besides a night of carnal enjoyment.

"Come here, little Ellie. You're too far away."

She scooted against him, curling into his embrace as if they had been doing this for months or years. He held her for long minutes, savoring the sense of peace. He wanted to make love to her. And he would, but he wanted a moment to pretend that she was his to keep.

At last, he ran a hand over her flank. "I need you," he said, the words unvarnished. "It eats me up. I can't stop thinking about you." Later he might regret his blunt honesty, but he wanted her to know how much he cared.

"I need you, too, Conor. Make love to me."

Sometimes sex was playful and sometimes it was erotic and sensuous. Tonight it was almost sacred. He moved into her, closing his eyes at the indescribable feeling of her tight passage clasping him and holding him and making wordless demands.

He would give her everything he had. But it might not be enough. Not enough to make her understand that life moved on and he wanted to move on with her. "Put your legs around my waist," he whispered. "I want more."

When she did as he asked, the resultant fit was perfect. He thrust again and again, as deeply as he could go, hard and fast, riding a wave he had no hope of beating. He heard Ellie cry out and knew he was free to take his own pleasure. But he held off a moment more. So he could imagine forever.

In the end, his climax caught him by surprise, ripping through his gut and demanding release.

He came forever, it seemed. And then everything was quiet.

What time was it? He had no clue. An hour might have passed. Or two. He was in heaven… floating on a cloud of bliss that would dissipate as soon as he opened his eyes.

Ellie was under him, their bodies still joined. He cleared his throat. “I can’t feel my legs,” he muttered. That fact might have been more alarming had he been less physically replete.

She pinched his thigh just below the buttock. Hard. “Still there,” she said.

He tried to summon the will to move, but it was a no-go. “Am I crushing you?”

“I’m tough. I can handle it.” Laughter lent wings to her words.

He smiled into her neck, inhaling her scent. “I hope you know CPR. If we do this again, I may black out from overexertion.”

"I thought you were the big, tough athlete."

He felt her fingers comb through his hair. He was in a bad way if such a simply, nonsexual touch could turn him inside out. "We all have our weak spots," he said. "Apparently, mine is you."

Fourteen

Apparently, mine is you. Ellie replayed his words in her head. What did they mean? Here she went again, overthinking things.

Deliberately, she let her mind wander, concentrating on each little piece of her current situation. The sheets on Conor's guest bed were top quality, smooth and cool even in summer. Conor's weight was comforting. She loved the feeling of connection, both mental and physical.

For this one moment in time, the two of them were in perfect accord. She was pretty sure she could feel his heart thumping against her breasts.

His hairy legs rubbed lazily against hers as if he might accidentally restart the fire. It wouldn't take much. Every time he gave her an orgasm, her greedy body started plotting for the next one.

"Are you sleepy?" she asked.

At last he shifted onto his back, yawning, leaving her bereft. "Give me fifteen minutes," he said, the words rough and low. He had one arm flung over his face. "And I'll be good to go again."

He was as good as his word. Twice…and once more during the night. The last time was somewhere around three in the morning. They finally decided they had to sleep, given that a baby was going to wake them up in a matter of hours.

Conor didn't bother asking her which half of the bed she wanted. He dragged her against his side, cuddling her close with one muscular arm.

She was sated and exhausted, but she didn't want to close her eyes when she had Conor all to herself. His breathing was slow and steady. She couldn't tell if he was actually asleep.

Was she ever going to tell him about Kevin? She knew there was no hope of anything serious unless she bared her soul. But a bared soul was so very raw and easily hurt. Conor's reaction was something she couldn't calculate.

He tugged a strand of her hair. "Go to sleep, Ell." The command was gravelly, his voice rough with fatigue. "Your son is not going to care that his mother has been awake all night."

"I know."

After another long silence, when she thought that surely Conor was asleep, he surprised her. "I wish Emory was mine. I wish I had been the first man to love you."

The giant boulder in her throat made it hard to speak. "Well, in a way you were," she said, tracing the silky line of hair near his navel. "It was puppy love, maybe. But still love, according to you."

"You know what I mean."

"Yes." He wished Kevin had never existed… had never wooed and married Ellie.

Conor tugged the light blanket over their shoulders. "Will you tell me about him…please? I want to know what he was like. He clearly had good taste in women."

The irony choked her. "I can't," she said, feeling the familiar tug of despair. "I can't, Conor. I'm sorry." Because if she told him the truth, he would walk away from her and never come back.

* * *

Conor slept in snatches until he heard the first sounds from Emory via the baby monitor. The toddler was used to him now and gave him a happy smile as Conor picked him up. After a clean diaper, the two men went in search of milk and cereal. Emory was hungry, so the meal was quick.

Conor, on the other hand, had no appetite at all. Until the middle of the night, he'd cruised on a high of endorphins, sure that he was winning Ellie over to his camp.

But it wasn't so. Things were the same as they had always been. Ellie couldn't bear to talk about her dead husband, and especially not to Conor.

When Emory's belly was full, Conor took him back to the bedroom and slid into bed beside Ellie. She stirred and lifted up on one elbow, swiping her hair from her face. She looked young and beautiful and confused.

"Why didn't you wake me?"

He shrugged. "I thought you could use the sleep. I'm always up early no matter how late I go to bed."

His oblique reference to their lovemaking was deliberate. He wanted to remind her they were good together. Incredibly incendiary, to be exact.

Ellie didn't appear to notice. She took Emory in her arms and nuzzled his neck. Suddenly, she must have realized that she was naked. "Ohmigosh, Conor. Bring me my robe."

"I'm sure he's seen you au naturel."

"Yes. But he was too young to understand. I don't want to scar him for life."

Conor rolled his eyes. "Do you worry about everything?"

"It's what mothers do. Comes with the territory."

He touched her arm. "My mother adores babies. And she knows you've had a difficult week. When I spoke to her yesterday, she offered to keep Emory for the morning so you and I can get away. Go for a drive. Walk in the mountains. Swim at Blackwoods Lake."

Ellie's mouth curved. "I'd forgotten about that. You and Kirby went skinny-dipping and left me on the shore. I was so mad at both of you."

"Well, it wasn't exactly appropriate as a group activity. But nothing's stopping us now."

"True. Does your mother really have time to babysit? Isn't Silver Beeches super busy this time of year?"

"It is. But Liam has insisted that Mom start

taking some time off. She ran this family and the family business solo for a great many years. She deserves to have some fun."

Ellie lifted an eyebrow. "Changing diapers is fun?"

Conor bumped noses with Emory, making him chortle with glee. "I think your mama's insulting you, little man."

Ellie hugged her son close. "I am not. But babies aren't easy."

"Trust me. Mom suggested a visit to Gavin and Cassidy's house so he can play with the twins. It will be an epic playdate. If you don't object, we'll let Mom take your car so we won't have to move the seat."

"It's lovely of her to offer, and I accept."

He cocked his head, studying her face in silence.

"What?" she asked. "What's the big deal?"

"I expected to get the Silver Glen version of the Spanish Inquisition. I had my answers all ready."

"Are you disappointed that I'm being amenable?"

He leaned over her and kissed the shell of her ear. "I *love* it when you're amenable." His lips found hers, and despite the squirmy bundle in her arms, they managed a breath-stealing kiss.

"Can you juggle him while I take a shower?"

Conor sighed inwardly. What he wanted was to climb back into bed with a naked delicious Ellie. "Sure. Hand him over."

An hour later, they headed out. With a list of instructions and a bulging diaper bag, Maeve Kavanagh drove away in Ellie's car, leaving her own at Conor's house. She was tickled pink to have the social and outgoing Emory in her care.

Conor pointed his vehicle in the opposite direction from town, soon accessing a narrow road he hadn't followed since he was a teenager. Ellie glanced around the leafy lane with a smile. "It's just like I remember it," she said. Two deep tire tracks in the dirt required all of his concentration to keep his low-slung car from getting hung up in the weeds.

When they rounded a curve, the tiny lake came into view, more of a pond really. A long-ago property owner had damned up the creek to create a swimming hole. The water was smooth, the mirrored surface reflecting a cloudless sky. Weeping willows fringed the entire oval except for a small area where someone had dumped a truckload of white sand to make a beach.

Conor hadn't kept up with who owned the acreage currently. But high school kids had come up here for years, making out and taking midnight swims. With an absence of No Trespassing signs, it was a harmless enough pursuit.

On the other hand, when two full-grown adults decided to ignore the fact that they had no right to be here, the law might be fuzzy. Conor parked in the shade of the largest willow and rolled down the windows. Though it wasn't yet noon, the temperature was merciless. The mountains of North Carolina were normally cool and pleasant even in summer, but a record heat wave had moved in with no relief in sight.

He and Ellie got out of the car and stood side by side, staring at the beckoning water.

Ellie wrinkled her nose. "I don't like the idea of wading in not knowing what I'm going to find underfoot."

"Then leave your sneakers on." He already wore his swim trunks. All he had to take off was his shirt.

Ellie, on the other hand, had donned a simple cotton sundress with an elastic waist. Presumably, her swimsuit was underneath. "I will."

He ruffled the ends of her ponytail. "I don't suppose I could get you to try the skinny-dipping thing..." He brushed the nape of her neck deliberately.

Ellie took a deep breath and closed her eyes. "Um, no. I have a healthy aversion to being arrested."

"Spoilsport." He opened the trunk of the car to take out their beach towels and a small cooler. When he turned back around, Ellie was standing there in a black bikini.

He dropped the cooler on his toe.

While he danced around and cursed under his breath, Ellie laughed at him, her face lit up from within. It struck him then, just how much this past year and a half had taken away her glow. Though he hadn't seen her in years, he knew that the adult Ellie would have possessed the same *joie de vivre* that had made young Ellie so irresistible.

Conor had never understood the point of putting a rail-thin woman in a bikini. To him, curves were far more appealing. Ellie had an hourglass figure that did full justice to her swimsuit.

He tried to hide his reaction, though if she peered too closely at the front of his trunks, she wouldn't have any doubts. After putting their things beneath the shade tree, he held out his hand. "Ready?"

Ellie gazed at him with a half smile. "Tell me the truth. Are we really trespassing?"

He put a hand over his heart. "I wouldn't lie to you. We're being wild and bad and totally irresponsible."

Her grin widened. "Exactly what the doctor ordered."

They waded hand in hand out into the deep. Ellie squealed and tried to turn back when the water felt cold against her hot skin. But Conor made her go the distance. When they were in up to their necks, he leaned into a backstroke and turned lazy circles around her. "Is that all you're going to do? Just stand there?"

She narrowed her eyes. "I'm getting acclimated," she said primly.

"Or you're being chicken." He splashed water in her face. "Are you chicken, Ellie?"

The flash of her eyes could have boiled the pond. "I am *not* chicken," she declared. "I'm here, aren't I?"

Were they still talking about swimming, or was their subconscious meandering around the subject of why Ellie trusted him with her body but not her secrets? "Yes," he said huskily. "You are. Come here, Ellie. Lean on me."

He tugged her by the hands out into the center of the pond. It was too deep to touch bottom, but he was a good swimmer. He moved his arms back and forth and kicked his legs strongly, keeping them afloat.

Ellie linked her wrists behind his neck. She was so close, he could see shades of amber in her irises. And the tiny white scar on her chin from where she wrecked her bike in fifth grade.

She destroyed him completely when she rested her head on his shoulder. "This was a wonderful idea. There's something about water that washes away everything bad."

"Are things still bad for you?" he asked quietly.

"No. Not especially. But life is complicated."

"Not like when we were kids."

"No."

He hesitated, belatedly realizing that he had wanted Ellie to share her darkest secrets with him, when he certainly hadn't been forthcoming about his. "I have a confession to make," he said. Beneath the water, their legs tangled, separated and tangled again.

With her breasts pressed up against him, it was difficult to focus, but this was important.

Ellie nuzzled his neck. "So serious. Is there a body buried up here somewhere?"

"You have a ghoulish imagination. Did anyone ever tell you that?"

She chuckled. "Maybe."

"No bodies," he said. The sun beat down on his head, making him dizzy. Or maybe it was the way Ellie clung to him as if she never wanted to let him go. He needed to hold her, but if he quit moving his arms, they would sink.

"You're being awfully mysterious," she said.

"It's no big secret, really. But when you asked me to help Kirby, I felt like a fraud."

She lifted her head, their lips almost touching. "I don't understand."

"You said I handled my disappointment about my ski career very well. But I didn't. I was angry as hell. And I spent a long time feeling sorry for myself."

"That's not what your family says."

"I'm a good actor. I was too proud to let anyone see how messed up I was."

"Oh, Conor. I didn't know."

"All I wanted to do was ski. I was such a cocky kid. I *knew* I was going to be the best in the world." Even now, the subject caught him in the throat. "I couldn't believe it when the doctor told me I couldn't compete anymore. Flying downhill was all I knew how to do. All I *wanted* to do."

"And then Kirby and I left." Her eyes were stricken.

"Yeah." He closed his eyes for a moment, afraid she would see how much he had suffered. A man didn't share those kinds of things. "So it hit me hard. I finished school and went on to college, but I was drifting. Taking over the ski lodge here at home was supposed to be a stopgap until I decided what I wanted to do with my life."

"And has it worked?"

When she looked into his eyes, it was as if she could see his sorry soul. Briefly, he regretted his revelation. But he wanted her to know that she was not the only one who had faced a loss of identity.

His arms were starting to tire, but his legs kept them afloat. "Turns out, I liked it. And being a part of Silver Glen, a part of the Kavanagh clan, has taught me what's important."

"But you still need to climb mountains to feel alive?"

He hadn't expected an outright attack. Then again, he of all people should know never to underestimate Ellie. She'd never let Kirby and Conor ride roughshod over her. And clearly, no one had ever told her that females were supposed to be the weaker sex.

"Low blow, Ell."

She nodded. "Yes. It was. But I'm trying to understand. You. My brother. You're smart men. It makes no sense."

"Life doesn't always make sense."

"Did you read that on a coffee mug somewhere?"

Conor was too relaxed to let her prod him. "Are we fighting?" he asked.

Her cute nose scrunched up in a suspicious frown. "Why do you want to know?"

"If we're fighting, it means we get to have makeup sex under that tree over there."

"Ah." Keeping one hand on his shoulder, she took the other one, slid it underwater and placed it smack on his goods. "Seems like we're on pretty good terms right now."

Conor choked and nearly drowned them both. "Um…"

"Um, what?" Her fingers were up to mischief.

"There's one big problem," he said.

"Oh?"

Less than sixty seconds of her brand of trouble and already she had him up and running. "*I* can't touch *you*," he complained. "Hardly seems fair."

She moved closer, wrapping her legs around his waist and kissing his chin and his neck. "I could do all the work."

He was tempted. Really tempted. But although he had spent three years on his high school swim team, he'd bet his last dime there wasn't a man alive who could keep his woman afloat while she was attacking him.

"How about a compromise?"

Fifteen

Ellie loved teasing Conor. Especially when he wanted the same thing she wanted. "I'm listening," she said.

"What if we move closer to shore so I can touch bottom?"

The buoyancy of the water made her feel light and free, but she was willing to be persuaded. "I like the idea of Conor Kavanagh being in over his head, but sure," she said.

He held her with one arm and swam with the other…only five or six strokes. When his feet found purchase, he kissed her. "Better. Much better," he said.

Beneath her fingertips, his skin was hot and

smooth. The sun shone down on them mercilessly. Feelings swamped her. So many feelings. Nostalgia hardly even made the list, though this was a spot she and Kirby and Conor had visited many times.

But it was more than that. Here, she felt closer to the essence of life. In some ways, this secluded miniature lake reminded her of the jungle. Not the specific features, but the scent of hot earth and the sensation of being one with nature.

She cried out when Conor slid a hand underneath her swimsuit bottom and touched her. Intimately. Where her body recognized him as a lover. "You said *under the tree*," she panted as he played with her devilishly.

Resting his forehead against hers, he muttered, "Decided it was too far. Can't wait. This works."

They were standing out in the pond in full view of anyone who happened to walk by. "But, Conor..."

He brushed her clitoris with his thumb as he read her mind. "No one's anywhere around. We'd hear a car driving down the lane. And worst-case scenario, if someone shows up out of the woods, he or she wouldn't really be able to see a thing."

Self-indulgence won out over prudishness. Barely.

Conor bit her earlobe. "Trust me, Ellie. I won't let you go."

"But how are we going to…"

He did some kind of contortion that allowed him to free his shaft. Taking her hand, he guided it to where he pulsed hard and ready. "I need you, Ell."

The fact that he didn't dress it up—that, and the raw urgency in his plea—destroyed her. "I'm here," she whispered.

When she played with him gently, his eyes squeezed shut and his face flushed. He made a noise. The guttural sound went straight to her sex, leaving her swollen and ready.

Conor didn't even remove her bikini bottom. Instead, he shoved aside the strip of fabric between her legs and pushed inside her. He seemed beyond speech, and that was okay with her, because mere words couldn't really capture the elemental joining.

Standing, and with the water as a buoyant cushion, he filled her completely, almost to the point of discomfort. His big hands cupped her bottom, lifting her into his thrusts.

She clung to him, dazed and crazed. Suddenly, it didn't matter if an entire brigade of onlookers appeared. The only thing that was real was Conor and his forceful possession.

They were wet and half-naked. Her fingernails dug into his shoulders. Arching her back, she moved with him, feeling his strength, his power, his utter focus on her and their joining.

She wanted to say *I love you.* To tell him how special he was. And how much he had healed the broken places in her heart. But instead, she buried her face in his neck and cried out when he sent her over the edge. The orgasm lasted for peak after peak. The pleasure was sharp and vicious, stripping away pretense.

Even as Conor found release in her body, she knew he had carved out a place in her heart and in her life. But in her future? The unlikelihood of that made her cling to him all the more. One more chance for bliss. One more day when she could pretend that their sexual chemistry was enough to erase everything else.

At last, when they were both breathing heavily and their muscles quivered, he staggered toward shore. At the last instant, he remembered to adjust their swimwear to a more modest orientation.

While Ellie stood, stunned and dripping in her sodden tennis shoes, Conor flipped out both of the big towels in a patch of grass and took her by the hand. “Five minutes,” he begged. “And then we’ll eat.”

They napped like children. Conor spooned her, his strong arms wrapped around her. It was the safest and most secure she had felt in a long, long time.

Eventually, hunger won out. They ate their picnic ravenously, laughing and talking and exchanging barbs. Beneath it all, sexual tension lurked. After another swim—a real swim this time—they made love on dry land. Ellie ended up on top. When she leaned forward to kiss him, Conor grabbed a handful of her damp hair, hair that was already drying in the hot sun.

He played with it, brushing it over her breasts, over his eyes. Inside her, he was big and hard. Physically, they were a perfect match, each intensely attuned to the other’s wants and desires.

“Conor,” she said impulsively. “I need to tell you something.”

His eyes darkened. "Not now, Ellie. Please. Today is about existing in the moment. No past. No future. Let's give ourselves a pass on real life. For once. You need a break. So do I."

With her hands on his taut shoulders, she nodded. "I'm going to be okay, Conor. You don't have to worry about me."

He grinned, lightening the mood. "You're way beyond okay, Ellie Porter. I give you a 9.7."

"How in the heck did I lose three tenths of a point?" She frowned.

Conor rolled them onto their sides, lifting her leg over his thigh as he thrust lazily. "One-tenth for stubbornness." He panted as time ran out for their spectacular finish. "One-tenth for being uptight."

She never did hear the last deduction. Conor groaned and came, taking her with him as he used his finger where their bodies joined to drive her wild.

In the aftermath, the afternoon was broken only by the sounds of their breathing and nature's horus. Bird calls. The wind in the trees overhead. Bullfrogs. Even the quick, distinctive visit of hummingbird wings.

It was one of those perfect moments when you want to distill time in a bottle and keep it forever. She stroked Conor's arm. "This has been a wonderful day. But I'm feeling the need to get home and see Emory."

"I understand."

They dressed in their original clothes, both of them damp and messy and definitely rumpled. Ellie grimaced. "I should have brought dry underwear. This swimsuit feels nasty."

Conor pulled a piece of grass from her hair. "Maybe we can snag a quick shower before we retrieve your son."

She punched his arm. "I know what you're thinking. And the answer is no. Separate showers. Short ones."

"Spoilsport." When he bent to gather up the towels he was smiling.

She finally remembered that Maeve would have to return Ellie's car. They couldn't pick up the baby in Conor's. So he sent his mother a text asking her to bring Emory home in a couple of hours and stay for dinner. Another quick text to the housekeeper, and the plans were set.

Ellie rested her head against the seat back as

they drove home. "It was a magical afternoon. I'll have to send your mother some flowers as a thank-you."

"When you get to know her better, you'll see that she's the one to thank you. My brothers have begun producing offspring, but slowly...too slowly for Mom. She probably won't be happy until each one of us has three or four."

"And do you want a lot of kids?"

"Hard to say. I was one of seven, but that's a tall order for the twenty-first century."

"It must have been fun...growing up in the Kavanagh family."

"Yeah. But it would have been even better if my dad had pulled his weight. And then when he disappeared..."

"Your mom had to do it all."

"I've never heard her complain."

"Because she's your mother. I'd love to have a big family, but not as a single mom. I don't know how she did it."

At Conor's house, they parked and unloaded things from the trunk. As they walked up the front steps, he put an arm around her waist. "I had fun today, Ellie."

Her feelings were close to the surface, but she managed a smile. “Me, too.” Happiness was a beautiful thing.

Kirby was waiting for them in the living room. He must have parked on the other side of the house.

“Hey, there,” she said. She went to hug him but stopped. Not because of her wet clothes, but because of the look on his face. “What’s wrong, Kirby?”

He didn’t rise when they walked into the room. That in itself alarmed her. Kirby had been a different man since Conor came back into their lives. Calmer. Happier. Now, her brother was white-faced, his hair unkempt, his hand fisted on the arm of the sofa.

She sat beside him and touched his knee. “Talk to me, Kirby. You’re scaring me.”

“It’s Grandpa,” he said. “He’s dead.”

Ellie’s vision grayed around the edges and she heard a buzzing in her ears. *Dead. Dead. Dead.* “I just spoke to him this morning. He was fine.” Her lips were numb. She had trouble forming the words.

Kirby scrubbed his hands over his face. “He

was watching TV in the recliner. We were chatting back and forth while I fixed his lunch. When I went into the den to tell him the meal was ready, he was gone."

"Oh, Kirby."

Conor watched, grim and incredulous as the twin siblings hugged each other. He wanted to go to Ellie and hold her, but now was not the time. She and Kirby were sharing their grief.

At last they separated. Conor handed Ellie a tissue but didn't say anything. He didn't know *what* to say. How was it fair for one woman to lose so much?

Kirby sat back, his head resting on the sofa. "They've taken his body to the funeral home. When they have him ready we'll go down there for you to say goodbye."

"And Mom and Dad?"

"They were both stunned. Dad got choked up on the phone. He's kicking himself for not coming home when we did. Now it's too late."

"Poor Daddy. What about the funeral? Will they fly home?"

"They're still discussing it, but my guess is no.

The logistics are phenomenally time-consuming, and as Dad said, it doesn't make sense to tackle those hurdles now when Grandpa is dead. I imagine they'll stay in Bolivia and when they finally move back next spring, we can have a brief private memorial service at the graveside."

Conor sat down across from them. "I am so very sorry. I liked Mr. Porter."

Kirby seemed more shaken than the situation warranted. "I'm a doctor, damn it. I keep asking myself if I missed something…if I should have taken him to the hospital this morning."

Conor stared at his two friends, hurting for them, feeling as if he were on shaky ground. "He died in his chair, Kirby. It sounds like a heart attack or a stroke. I know it's hard for you and your family, but if you think about it, we should all be so lucky to go that peacefully."

Neither sibling said much after that. He wondered if he had been too blunt with them. Conor stepped out of the room briefly to check in with his mom. She said Emory was waking from his nap and they would be on their way soon. Conor told Maeve what had happened and asked her to keep Emory a little longer.

When Conor returned to the dining room, Kirby was holding Ellie in his arms and they were both crying. Hell.

Quietly, he backed away and went to sit on the front porch.

When Ellie at last came to find him, almost two hours had passed. "We're going to the funeral home," she said. "But I don't know what to do about Emory."

"It's all taken care of. No worries. Would you like me to come with you?"

Ellie seemed smaller and quieter, as if a light had been snuffed out. "It's not necessary."

He stood up and cradled her to his chest. "I phrased that wrong. *May* I come with you? I really want to."

She nodded, sniffing against chest. "I'd like that."

They took separate cars to the funeral home. Conor had convinced Kirby to pack a bag and come up to Conor's house afterward. There was no reason for Kirby to stay alone down at Mr. Porter's house and grieve.

None of them felt much like eating dinner, but

there was a little café in town where they could get soup and a sandwich afterward.

Conor had known the funeral home director most of his life. The man was professional and kind. Luckily, there were no other services that evening, so the place was quiet. Too quiet, maybe. It was hard to escape the aura of death and sadness.

Mr. Porter's body was draped in a sheet. Kirby and Ellie would have to make decisions about clothes and caskets and everything else in the morning. For now, it was time for a very private farewell.

Ellie touched the old man's forehead. "Goodbye, Grandpa. I'll miss you."

Conor had his left arm around her waist. Kirby held her left hand. As a trio, they had seen and survived a lot of ups and downs. Conor wished he could spare both of them this pain. They had survived so much. But it wasn't his call.

Ellie cried, silent tears that ran down her face and dripped onto her dress. "We should have come home sooner. We knew he wasn't doing well."

Her words made Kirby blanch.

Conor shook his head. "You didn't really have

that choice. And your grandfather knew that. Until Kirby was on the mend, your grandfather would have wanted the two of you to spend time together."

"I suppose." She touched the body again, smoothing a lock of white hair. "He was so much fun when we were kids. After my grandmother died, he came to Bolivia a few times. He liked to travel, but he used to laugh and say that his old body didn't."

Conor had to take his cues from Kirby. At last Ellie's brother steered her away. "We have a lot to do tomorrow, Ell. Let's grab a bite to eat and go home to bed."

"Home?" She looked panicked.

"To Conor's, I mean."

"Oh...yes."

During the quick meal they consumed, the two men talked of generalities. Ellie said nothing, though she did eat all of her tomato soup and chicken sandwich.

Afterward, Kirby went to the empty Porter house to pack up his things.

When Ellie and Conor got to Conor's house, Maeve was already there with Emory. Conor's mother extracted Emory from his car seat and handed him over to Ellie. Then she hugged both Ellie and Emory. "Your son is a delight. And he's so smart."

For the first time that day, Ellie smiled. "Well, I think so, but I'm his mom, so I'm supposed to say that."

Maeve sobered. "I am so sorry to hear about your grandfather. I knew Mr. Porter. Most of Silver Glen did. He was well respected and much loved. Please accept my sympathies."

Ellie hugged Emory, her eyes damp. "Thank you, Mrs. Kavanagh. If you all will excuse me, I need to get Emory ready for bed."

When she walked into the house, Conor shrugged. Maeve was the first to speak. "Are you in love with that girl?"

"Mom!" Conor actually felt his ears turning red.

"Okay," she said, sighing. "I'll wait until you want to talk about her. I'm headed home."

Conor nodded in relief. "Kirby will be here in a few minutes. He and Ellie have some decisions to make. I'll keep you posted."

Maeve had no sooner driven away than Kirby showed up. He got out of his car with only a slight limp, perhaps due to stress and fatigue. In one hand he carried a small suitcase. He couldn't manage a smile as he walked up the front steps with Conor. "Where's Ellie?" he asked.

Conor held the door for him. "Putting the baby to bed. You want a beer?"

Kirby shook his head. "I'd like a shower if you don't mind."

"I'll show you the other guest room." Once Conor had pointed out all the amenities to his friend, he stopped in the open door on his way out. "I'm sorry, Kirby. Really sorry."

Kirby shook his head. "I never saw it coming down like this. I guess I need to make up my mind about those job offers."

Conor's stomach pitched at the implications of that statement. "Won't you have to deal with the house?"

"No. Dad and Mom will do that when they come back in the spring. I'll turn the utilities off, pay bills, you know...none of that will take more than a few days."

"What are you telling me, Kirby?"

"Ellie and I will be leaving Silver Glen sooner rather than later."

Sixteen

Conor lay awake for hours. He wanted Ellie in his bed, or he wanted to be in hers. Not for sex, though he thought about that with every other breath. He wanted to comfort her…to hold her…to promise her that she was going to get through this.

He and Kirby had stayed up until the wee hours…talking…occasionally laughing…cementing the bond that had grown since Kirby's return. They both shared a concern for Ellie's well-being. Though Ellie hadn't exhibited any lasting signs from her hospital stay, Mr. Porter's death was the emotional equivalent of "piling on."

Ellie was strong. But even the strongest trees break when the storms are bad.

Conor had made arrangements with his housekeeper to have a hearty breakfast ready at nine o'clock. Kirby and Ellie and Emory beat Conor to the table and were waiting for him.

Kirby looked pretty good for a man who hadn't slept much. "Thanks for the bed and the meal, Conor."

"It's the least I can do."

Ellie looked at him beseechingly. "I don't want to leave Emory again today. Would you mind coming with us to the funeral home and playing with him in the lobby?"

"Of course not." He reached across the table and touched her hand, not caring that Kirby was watching. "Did you sleep?"

Ellie nodded. "Yes." She looked at her brother and at Conor. "I'm okay, guys. You can stand down." Her smile reassured him, but he noticed she was paler than usual. And in her eyes he saw traces of that same vulnerability that worried him.

Fortunately, the decisions at the funeral home didn't take long. Ellie's eyes were red rimmed when they came out of the consultation room, but she seemed calm. "We're done," she said, taking Emory from him.

"What now?"

"The funeral will be tomorrow evening. The notice has already gone to the newspaper. We planned a very simple service."

Kirby took Ellie's arm. "Will it bother you if we all go over to Grandpa's house? We both could pack up our things. Conor says we're welcome to stay with him and, frankly, I want to, because the house without Grandpa is way too sad and empty."

"I agree."

While Kirby took care of a few last details with the funeral home concerning payment, Ellie and Emory sat in a nearby conversation area furnished with comfortable chairs. Emory was beginning to fuss, no doubt because he was hungry.

Conor leaned forward with his elbows on his knees and forced Ellie to look him straight in the eyes. "I'm sorry, Ellie. Really sorry."

Her smile this time was more of a grimace. "We were having such a beautiful day…"

He caressed her cheek with the back of his hand. "We were. I hope you won't let what happened ruin your memories of yesterday. I won't forget it. Ever."

"Why?" Her eyes were huge.

"Because it was fun and crazy and amazing."

"It was, wasn't it?"

He leaned forward, almost kissing her, when they both remembered where they were.

He jerked backward.

Ellie turned red. "Bad timing," she muttered.

"Sorry." He was chagrined that his need for her could make him stupid. "I don't know what I was thinking."

"The same thing I was, I suppose. That we're damned good together in bed."

He clapped his hands over Emory's ears. "Ellie. Watch your mouth."

"Kirby's his uncle. I'm sure he's heard worse."

Kirby walked up and sat down beside them. "I heard my name being taken in vain. Not fair when I can't defend myself."

Ellie jumped to her feet. "Don't get comfortable. I don't know about you, but funeral homes give me the creeps. Let's get out of here."

By nine that evening, Kirby and Ellie were firmly ensconced in Conor's home. He found himself smiling for no particular reason except that he liked having them all beneath his roof.

Kirby took himself off to bed early. When Ellie disappeared with the baby to put him to bed, Conor grabbed a shower and changed into a pair of cotton sleep pants. Under the circumstances, he wasn't going to wander nude around his house.

He had a feeling that his troubled thoughts were going to keep him awake yet again. Knowing that Kirby and Ellie no longer had a reason to stay in Silver Glen was both disturbing and galvanizing. He needed to do something. Say something.

But he kept coming back to his original stumbling block. Once before, Ellie had asked him to choose her over his skiing and he hadn't been able to do it. Would she expect him now to give up everything he loved to be with her?

Could he push for some kind of relationship with her knowing that Kevin's memory would always linger between them like an unwelcome third wheel? It was natural for a wife to grieve her husband. But for how long? Forever? Would Conor regret pushing the issue if all he could have was her body and her friendship?

Staring into a cup of decaf coffee, he made a

decision. He and Ellie were friends. Good friends. Better than they had been in the last decade. Though it would be incredibly hard, he was going to let her go without a fight.

He wanted a woman whose heart was hers to give. He needed the kind of relationship his four older brothers had found. Ellie was one in a million. One day, when she managed to forget the tragedies of the past, she would be ready to move on.

But that time had not yet come.

With a splitting headache and a crushing pain in his chest, he placed the empty cup in the sink and turned out all the lights.

Padding barefoot down the hall to his bedroom, he stopped in shock just inside the door. Ellie was waiting for him. She perched on the side of his bed wearing a chaste blue knit gown that was not designed to be remotely sexy.

Even the conventional garment flattered her. Her hair fell around her shoulders, making her look young and vulnerable.

"Ellie." That was smooth. But he was off his game. How was he supposed to act around the woman he wanted with every cell in his body?

Her hands twisted in her lap. "I missed you last

night," she said, her gaze dark and, for once, impossible to read. "Will you sleep with me?"

Hell, yes. "Of course." He sat down beside her and took one of her hands in his. "Do you need anything? Warm milk? Hot cocoa? A snack?"

She managed a smile. "All I need is you."

He slid a hand behind her neck and pulled her in for a slow kiss. He tried to give her gentleness and patience. What he received in return was a kick to the gut. Raw passion. Unbridled desire.

Hand in hand, they returned to her room. "I'll hold you while you sleep."

She faced him, the broad expanse of the mattress between them. "That isn't enough."

"Ellie, I..." He ran his hands through his hair. Surely he deserved this one last time with her before she went away. But was it right? "You're in the midst of a crisis," he said.

"Life and death and change, Conor. What else is there? I'd rather be with you tonight than anywhere else in the world."

She stood there, bold and brave, breaking his heart with her almost visible aura of valor in the face of overwhelming odds.

"Then you have me," he said. "Take off your gown."

* * *

Ellie spared a moment to wonder if Conor thought she was being flippant about her grandfather's passing. She wasn't. Losing her only surviving grandparent was inevitable, but she hadn't been ready. No one ever was. She'd thought they had months, not days, to hear stories and swap hugs and be a family.

Now there was one less piece of her. One more broken spot that had to be glued back together.

She undressed, not because Conor had demanded it, but because she wanted to feel his naked skin against hers. Grief hovered in the wings, crushing and undeniable. But tonight she would hold it at bay, sheltered in Conor's embrace.

With the lights out, pale moonlight streamed through a crack in the drapes. She went to the window and pushed back the heavy fabric, needing to see evidence of eternity. "Do you mind?" she asked.

"No. We're invisible in the dark and, besides, there's no one around. Come to bed, Ellie."

They met in the center of the mattress on their knees. He smoothed her hair, his breath warm on her cheek.

"You make me happy, Conor," she whispered. There was so much more to say than that, but for tonight it was enough.

"I'm glad."

She felt him pressed close to her, chest to breasts, thigh to thigh. His rigid sex thrust against her belly, eager and importunate. Reaching between them, she took him in her hand, noting the sharp hiss of his breath.

"I love how you feel," she murmured, still dazzled by the rightness of being with him this way.

He groaned and laughed. "It's pretty good from this side, too." He cupped her breasts. "You have the most amazing body, Ellie. Not that I'm not crazy about your mind, but damn, woman."

When he pinched her nipples, she moved into him, wanting to be closer and closer still. "Don't make me wait tonight," she pleaded.

"Not a problem."

After that, words became unnecessary. They fell onto the bed with soft mutters and choked laughter, so attuned to each other that she knew when he paused to debate the logistics. "Do you need a map?"

He moved behind her instantly and dragged a

couple of pillows beneath her as she moved onto her hands and knees. "You're such a smart-ass, Ellie."

The laughter in his voice relaxed her, made her soft with yearning. As he entered her from behind, she felt his fingers on the nape of her neck. The innocent caress was in counterpoint with the primeval way he possessed her. His body staked a claim.

Closing her eyes, she buried her face in the pillow. Yesterday she had been on the brink of taking a chance…of telling him that she loved him… of confessing her secrets and her pain. But she'd thought she had more time. It was a hard lesson to learn. The only certain moments were in the now.

In the past few weeks, Kirby had spent numerous hours narrowing down his choice of hospitals. He was ready to make a decision. Which meant that soon, he and Ellie and Emory would be moving.

Her heart was breaking.

Conor eased out of her body and suddenly flipped her onto her back. "I need to see your face. You left me, didn't you?"

"I'm sorry," she said. "I was thinking about things."

He moved between her thighs and entered her a second time. "Don't think. Just feel."

Conor loved her gently and thoroughly, shuddering in her arms as he finished. Ellie's climax was more of a gentle swell and a gasped breath. In the aftermath, he wrapped her in his arms and kissed her temple. "I've got you, Ellie. Go to sleep."

The funeral was both a pleasure and an endurance test. Many more people showed up than she and Kirby had expected. Her grandfather had lived in Silver Glen most of his life. Townspeople came by, even those who didn't know Kirby and Ellie personally.

The Kavanagh clan turned out in full force, demonstrating their support. Since Emory wasn't the only child needing to be entertained, two college students home for the summer had been commandeered to babysit in a small room near the chapel where the service was to be held.

Through it all, Conor stood at Ellie's side. His comforting presence gave her strength. He introduced her to strangers and brought her water and tissues and generally made himself indispensable.

Kirby held court in an opposite corner. They had decided it made sense to divide and conquer. They had been receiving friends for over two hours, and she worried about her brother's stamina.

When she mentioned as much to Conor in a low voice, he shook his head and muttered in her ear. "I know Kirby. He won't sit down even if you ask him to. But don't worry. I'll keep an eye on him."

At last, it was time for the service. Ellie sat in the front row, Kirby and Conor flanking her. Though the minister was articulate and kind and had lovely things to say about Mr. Porter, Ellie blanked out.

Until that instant, she hadn't taken stock of the fact that this was her first funeral since Kevin's. It hit her suddenly, an overwhelming feeling as if she were drowning.

Sweat dampened her forehead and she wanted to gasp for breath. But there were rows and rows of people behind her. She could feel their eyes on her back. She gripped Conor's hand until her fingernails dug into his palm.

At last, it was over. The family was escorted out a side door. Ellie saw the black hearse, the black limo. The one she had ridden in with Kevin's parents on the way to the cemetery.

She tried to speak. But nausea rose in her throat. "I…Conor…"

Blackness swirled and shrouded her until the world disappeared.

Seventeen

Conor caught her before she hit the ground.

Kirby cursed.

"I'll take her home," Conor said.

Kirby nodded, his worried gaze on his sister's limp body in Conor's arms. "The graveside service won't take long. I'll be right behind you…or as soon as I can."

Conor's car was parked not far away. Opening the passenger door, he reclined the seat, set Ellie down carefully and belted her in after smoothing the skirt of her knee-length black dress. Moments later, when he started the engine, Ellie roused and sat up.

She put her hand over his on the gearshift. "Conor. Tell me what happened."

"You fainted. I'm taking you home."

"No, you're not." She reached for the door handle, unlocking it before he could stop her. "I can't let Kirby go to the cemetery on his own."

Fury blasted through Conor's calm. "Hell, Ellie. You don't have to take care of the whole entire world. Somebody needs to take care of *you* for a change. And like it or not, today, that somebody is me."

She gaped at him as if he had sprouted an extra head. "You're yelling at me."

"Damn straight I am. Now sit still and do what I tell you to do."

Ellie collapsed in her seat, tearing leaking from the corners of her eyes.

Shit. "I'm sorry," he said hoarsely. "I know this is a tough day. But you're scaring me to death. People have heart attacks from stress, Ellie. Or complete mental breakdowns."

She didn't say a word.

He leaned his forehead on the steering wheel and said a prayer for patience. "I won't make you leave," he muttered. "If you're set on going to the cemetery."

Still the tears fell, slowly, painfully. As if something had broken and couldn't be fixed.

She turned her head toward him, face wet, expression quietly determined. "I want to go to the cemetery. But not in the limo. In your car. Will you go tell Kirby?"

"Do you want him to ride with us?"

She nodded, sniffing. "Yes, please."

Conor fetched Kirby and the two men climbed into the car without speaking, Conor behind the steering wheel, Kirby in the backseat. The cemetery wasn't far. A much smaller subset of mourners had come for this portion of the service. Many of them were Kavanaghs.

The day was warm but drizzly. Most people huddled beneath the green awning that flanked the burial spot. Conor kept a hand on Ellie the entire time. Her gaze was fixed on the flower-draped casket.

As promised, the ceremony was brief. Soon, after shaking hands and speaking with a few more people, it was time to go. Maeve had taken Emory with her to give Kirby and Ellie some time to change clothes and regroup.

Conor drove home, his gut in turmoil. Neither of his passengers spoke. When they reached the house, Ellie fled from the car. There was no other word for it.

Kirby and Conor climbed out and stared at each other.

"She'll be fine," Kirby said.

For the first time, Conor could tell he was lying.

After changing into jeans and a comfortable cotton button-down, Conor grabbed a sandwich. People had brought food to the house…enough to feed a small country. Conor liked living in a place where community was important. He'd watched as Kirby and Ellie reminisced with old friends and met cordial strangers. The Porter twins were wrapped in a cocoon of concern whether they realized it or not.

At last, he couldn't stand it. He had to check on Ellie. Giving her space seemed like the smart thing to do right now, but his gut was telling him there was more going on with Ellie than met the eye. Sadly, he had a feeling he knew what it was.

All of the funeral stuff must have brought back Kevin's death.

Her bedroom door was open. No Ellie. She wasn't in the living room, either. Kirby, however, was sacked out facedown on the sofa. Conor exited as silently as he had come. His buddy needed the rest.

It was another ten minutes before he found Ellie…on the deck that extended from the back of the house. Conor had plans to put in a swimming pool and hot tub, but he hadn't gotten that far yet.

He had, however, invested in a collection of cushioned deck furniture. Some nights, he and a few poker buddies played out here and watched the sunset. Other times, Conor simply liked to sit as the evening waned and be alone with his thoughts.

Ellie had chosen a lounge chair, though it was a good bet she wasn't relaxed. She had her knees pulled up to her chest with her arms circling them. To Conor, the posture looked defensive.

Dragging a chair closer without an invitation, he felt his heart break when he saw that she was crying, sobbing, in fact.

He picked her up and sat back down on the

chaise with her, his legs outstretched, Ellie curled in a ball of misery against this chest.

For a long time, he let her cry it out. They had nowhere to go, and tears were often cathartic. Eventually, however, he felt her go soft in his arms…heard the ragged cadence of her breathing as she exhausted herself.

Choosing his words carefully, he stroked her hair as he spoke. "Your grandfather wouldn't want you to do this, Ell. He'd want you to be happy."

She scrubbed a hand over her face and gave a little hiccupping sigh. "I'm not crying for Grandpa," she said.

"You're not?" Conor frowned.

"Well, I'm sad. I'll miss him a lot. But he lived a good life, and with the dementia accelerating, he faced a difficult road ahead. Now he's whole. And with my grandmother."

"Then why are you so upset? Why the tears, Ell? For Kevin? Did today bring it all back? Is that it?"

She stared at him, her expression guarded. "Yes. But not in the way you're thinking."

"It's understandable," he said gruffly, almost unable to look at her, because it hurt so damned much to know she still loved her dead husband.

"It hasn't been that long since you buried him. Healing takes time." More time than Conor had.

Shaking her head, she flipped her hair behind her shoulders. The simple navy top she wore emphasized her pallor. "I shed all my tears for Kevin a long time ago. Today I was crying for you."

He stared at her. "I don't know what you mean."

"When we came home from the lake and Kirby was sitting there with such a terrible look on his face…waiting to tell me bad news…I realized that one day that same scenario may unfold. Only Kirby will be telling me about you. I've been strong and resilient and all those things they tell me I'm supposed to be. But, oh, Conor…if you died, I couldn't bear it."

She used the hem of her shirt to dry her face. The childish action made him want to smile, but this confrontation was too important.

"That won't happen," he said firmly.

Her jaw firmed mutinously. "You don't know for certain."

"I do," he said. "Because I canceled my trip yesterday."

She gaped at him. "Why?"

Why, indeed. Here came the hard part. In fact,

he couldn't be this close to her and say it. So he levered himself up from the lounger and paced the deck. "You and I have differing opinions on the mountain-climbing thing, Ellie. I see it as an adventure. You see it as a death sentence. I may not agree with you, but I certainly understand why you feel that way."

She scooted back into her original position, resting her chin on her knees. "I still don't get why you canceled."

He shrugged. "Because I love you." The words fell like stones from his mouth. He held up a hand. "Don't say anything. Not a word. I know it's too soon and you still love Kevin. I know all that. But I love you too much to put you through any more pain. So the trip is off."

Ellie was astonished and deeply moved. To hear that Conor cared enough about her to give up something so important to him was utterly precious and very emotional.

But she had used up her tears.

The time had come to be honest with Conor. He deserved the truth, even if it put her in a bad light...even if it changed his opinion of her.

She wouldn't tell him she loved him. Not yet. Because he needed to understand the whole picture. She had kept things from him intentionally. To protect herself. To survive. To keep him at a distance.

But Conor had thrown down the gauntlet. He had been as honest as a man can be. It was up to her to match his courage.

"You've asked me again and again to open up to you or to Kirby about my feelings. To talk about Kevin's death. Both of you believe that I haven't dealt with what happened, and you're right. I suppose my hospitalization last week proved that. I didn't completely snap, but I definitely came unglued. Lucky for me, I had very good care. Although it may surprise you, I did share things with the doctor."

Conor sat down in a chair, his hands on his knees. "I'm so glad."

"It was hard. I won't lie. But I knew that if I could tell a stranger, I could eventually tell you."

"You don't have to. It's been a difficult day."

"I *want* to," she said.

Conor sat and waited. She liked that about him.

His calm strength. His utterly unbreakable commitment to those he loved.

She searched her brain, looking for the perfect place to start. But the story was fragmented and sad and ugly. So one spot was as good as another. "Kevin and I were having trouble," she said.

"I see."

"It had been going on for far too long. We'd been married four years when he died. The first two were good...the last two not so much."

"Where did you meet?"

"In Buenos Aires. His father was Argentinian, his mother American. So Kevin straddled both cultures. He was sophisticated and well-traveled and never met a stranger. I was twenty-four. He was seven years older. He dazzled me."

"Did your parents approve?"

"I think so. He came from a good family. Had a great job. The two of us were head over heels in love."

"So what happened?"

"He wasn't cut out to be monogamous...or that's what he told me. When the cheating started, I questioned myself. I know, looking back, that I was not thinking clearly. But all I had to go by was my parents' marriage. They were—and still are—devoted to each other. I began to ask myself if I had failed Kevin somehow."

"Please tell me you know that's a pile of crap."

Conor's indignation soothed her nerves.

"I do now. But instead of addressing the infidelity directly, I begged him to go to marriage counseling." Remembering those sessions made her cringe inside. "Kevin was an amazing chameleon. He could wring emotion from an audience with a bald-faced lie and no one ever questioned him. The therapist we were seeing told me I was young and naive and I needed to learn how to trust my husband and not be so insecure."

Conor's vicious curse and look of incredulity was satisfying. Though the worst was yet to come. He shook his head. "That's almost criminal."

"You can see why I began to wonder if the problem was me. But in the end, I discovered that Kevin was a serial cheater. Things came to a head when I found out that one woman he'd been seeing regularly was also going on the Aconcagua trip."

"Damn."

"Yep. I told him I was finished. That I was going to file for divorce."

"And he agreed?"

"No. He said I was being childish and that there was no need for us to break up our marriage. That men were different from women and they needed variety. But I was still his wife. Blah, blah, blah…"

"Please tell me you punched the guy."

"Maybe if I had, I would feel better about all this. But no."

"And you didn't tell anyone?"

"I was too ashamed. I had always been the *smart* girl. It was humbling to know I had been taken in by a man whose personality and integrity were nothing more than smoke and mirrors." She paused, her throat tightening. "I moved out."

Conor was confused. Foreboding settled in his gut. By all rights, this story should be making him feel relieved. Instead, his skin crawled.

"So you moved out," he said slowly. "Good for you."

Ellie nibbled one of her fingernails. He'd never seen her do that. "Good in theory. Kevin was furious. I packed my things while he was at work one day. When he came home to an empty house, he went ballistic. He hired a detective, and in less than twenty-four hours Kevin was on my doorstep."

"What did he say?"

"His performance was Oscar-worthy. Contrition. Repentance. Begging for another chance."

"You didn't."

"I did. To me, marriage vows were sacred. If he was genuinely willing to change, I felt duty-bound to try again."

"Aw, hell, Ellie." He knew something was coming he didn't want to hear. "What did you do?"

"He asked to come in. I let him. And he forced himself on me. Repeatedly."

Conor felt nausea rise in his throat. "He raped you."

"He was my husband." She was so pale he was worried that she might faint again.

"Husband or not, Ellie, Kevin had no right to your body if you said no."

"He didn't see it that way. And he had an ace in the hole. He knew if I got pregnant that I would never leave him. So he didn't use protection."

Conor felt as if he were being ripped apart from the inside out. He didn't want the rest of Ellie's halting confession. He couldn't handle it. But he had no choice.

"What happened then?"

"When he fell asleep, I ran away."

"To Kirby's place?"

"I wanted to…so badly. But Kirby and Kevin were going on the Aconcagua trip together in little over a week. I didn't want there to be bad blood between them. A girlfriend offered me her couch. Since her boyfriend was a policeman, I felt relatively safe."

"And Kevin?"

"I have no idea if he tried to find me or not. I didn't go to work. I didn't go out. My friend wanted me to press charges. But I wouldn't agree. I'm not sure what I thought I was going to do. I was in shock, I guess."

"Thank God, you had someone looking out for you."

"Yes. I was lucky."

"What happened next?"

"I never saw Kevin again. The next I knew of him was when I got word that he had fallen and died. And that Kirby was stranded."

Holy God. This was far worse than finding out

Ellie was pining for a lost love. He was dumbfounded and struggling to process the dreadful details. She'd been raped, widowed and almost lost her brother.

"Who got in touch with you?"

"I felt safe because Kevin was on the mountain. So I went home to get some more clothes and larger items I'd had to leave behind. I had recovered enough mentally to know what he had done to me. I was prepared to go back to my apartment and press charges as soon as he returned. While I was at the house, the phone rang and rang. I finally answered it. That's when I heard what had happened." She shook her head, her expression bemused. "Three weeks later I found out I was pregnant."

Conor hunched his shoulders and searched for words. No wonder she hadn't wanted to talk about it. "Did you ever tell Kirby and your parents?"

She shrugged. "No. Kirby has had enough to deal with without juggling my problems. And the truth would have killed my parents."

"I don't know what to say, Ellie. I wish he was alive so I could throttle him."

Her smile was weak. "You said you loved me.

But you need to hear me out before you say it again."

"It's not the kind of thing a man takes back in fifteen minutes."

His humor was lost on her. "Conor." She looked out over the valley, almost as if she had forgotten he was there.

"Yes, Ellie?"

"When I hung up the phone…after hearing that Kevin was dead, I did something terrible."

He couldn't let her go on. Not without touching her. Returning to where she sat, he picked her up, even as she struggled to get free, and sat down, pulling her between the vee of his thighs so her back was against his chest.

"Okay, my love. Tell me this terrible thing you did."

She waited so long he thought she had changed her mind. Her fingers linked with his, playing with the gold signet ring on his right hand. Finally, she spoke. "I stood there in our house…the place I never wanted to see again, and I wasn't sad. I wasn't devastated. I wasn't even upset."

He kissed the back of her hair. "You were likely in shock, but go ahead."

She half turned, staring up at him with tragic eyes. "I was relieved, Conor. What kind of person is *relieved* to hear someone has died?"

A year and a half. Eighteen months. Longer by now. All this time she had borne the weight of her guilt. Even as she nursed her brother back to health…even as she endured labor and sleep deprivation and learned how to be a good mother… all that time his sweet Ellie had tortured herself.

He cupped her face in his hands and kissed her nose. "You are such a drama queen. If you were expecting me to throw you out of my house or demand that you dress in sackcloth and ashes, you're going to be sadly disappointed."

The look of shock on her face was priceless. Not for anything in the world would he let her know how horrified he was by what she had experienced. His job was to give her normalcy…and indirect absolution. Smiling, though it was an effort to tamp down his anger at her worthless dead husband, he pulled her to her feet.

"I love you," he said, the words steady. "Nothing you told me just now changes that. Nothing ever will."

Ellie gazed at him with an expression that defied description. She had kept her emotions under such tight lock and key it was no wonder she'd stumbled recently. No one could keep such painful secrets indefinitely. But Ellie had tried.

Her arms hung at her sides, though his were around her shoulders. "I made a terrible mistake, Conor. How can I ever trust my judgment again?"

Her question was valid. But he had the answer.

"Tell me something, Ellie. When you and Kirby came back to Silver Glen, what did you think when you saw me?"

"Ah…" The muscles in her throat worked. "I… uh…"

"You felt a spark, didn't you? A small, warm remembrance of the past."

She licked her lips. "Yes."

He could barely hear the syllable. Gathering her into his arms, he lifted her onto her toes and kissed her until they were both breathless. "We had something, Ellie. All those years ago. It was a seed, I think. A seed that contained the possibility of something pretty wonderful. But things happened. Life separated us. So the seed never germinated."

"Are you sure you aren't a botanist?"

Her sass reassured him. If she could spar with him, she was going to be okay. "I'm serious. If you had stayed in South America…if you'd had a happy marriage…you and I would have been nothing but a memory."

"And now?"

Joy rose in his chest. And a surge of adrenaline stronger than any he'd ever experienced while skiing or climbing a mountain. "Now, I'm going to fertilize the hell out of that thing. I'm going to tell you I love you every day of your life. I'm going to make love to you every night so that we're both haggard from lack of sleep. God willing, and with your agreement, I'm going to give little Emory a few siblings."

"All that from a seed?" Her eyes were shining with happiness, not tears.

"It's our own little miracle."

She slid her hands around his neck, playing with his ears, stroking his nape. "I don't think Kirby really wants to go to Miami. He asked me what I thought about him opening a clinic here…one that caters to children with special needs. And I've been thinking that Silver Glen might need an international visitor center." She rested her head on his shoulder. "I love you with all my heart, Conor Kavanagh."

He had waited a long time to hear it. Now that the moment had come, his knees were embarrassingly weak. "No take backs."

Lifting her by the waist, he set her on the teak picnic table so he could better reach her mouth. He kissed her hard, his hands tangled in her beautiful hair as he held her head and angled her lips to his.

"Marry me," he muttered. "Let me adopt Emory."

"Yes." She smothered his face with kisses, her light happy laughter more gratifying to him than all the gold medals in the world.

"I wonder if we could send Kirby up to the Silver Beeches Lodge to spend the night."

"Conor!" She punched his arm. "You'd throw your best friend to the wolves just to have sex with me?"

"Loud sex. Noisy sex. Kitchen-table sex. And yes, I would. Though a room at a five-star hotel is hardly a punishment."

She wrapped her legs around his waist, leaning back on her hands. "If we're nice to him, he might be willing to keep Emory while we go on our honeymoon."

Conor's eyes glazed over. He was hard and ready. And he wanted Ellie. When he got her in bed, he'd never let her go. "Works for me," he said.

"I love you, Conor."

It was only the second time she had said it. He didn't think the words would ever get old. Her smile was everything that was Ellie. Sweet. Sexy. Funny. And his. No shadows. No ghosts. Only a future for them to explore together.

"I love you, too, my gorgeous, wonderful best friend." He kissed the spot beneath her ear that was supersensitive.

"Do you think Kirby will be surprised?"

"I doubt it. Your brother is a very smart man." He pulled her to her feet. "Let's go tell him the good news."

As they walked into the house, it hit him hard. Happiness. Contentment. Sheer euphoria. He was *home*. And Ellie Porter was finally his.

She looked up at him, mischief on her face. "But we're still having sex later, right? Even if we have to be quiet?"

"You can count on it, Ellie. You can count on it."

* * * * *